# ALEXANDRA

Also by Scott O'Dell

# ALEXANDRA

Scott O'Dell

Houghton Mifflin Company
Boston 1984

*Library of Congress Cataloging in Publication Data*

O'Dell, Scott, 1903–
  Alexandra.

  Summary: While helping her crippled grandfather by
diving for sponges from the family boat after the death
of her diver father, Alexandra discovers that someone is
using their sponges as a hiding-place for smuggled cocaine.
  [1. Greek Americans—Fiction.  2. Sponge fisheries—
Fiction.  3. Florida—Fiction.  4. Grandfathers—Fiction.
5. Smuggling—Fiction]  I. Title.
PZ7.O237A  1984     [Fic.]      83-26590
ISBN 0-395-35571-0

Printed in the United States of America

Q  10  9  8  7  6  5  4  3  2  1

To
Matilda Welter,
Editor and Friend

# ALEXANDRA

1

The day dawned clear and quiet, but now a wind was rising out of the Gulf, above the reefs at Anclote Key. We heard it in the palm trees as we sat down to supper. At first it was only a whisper, scarcely that — more like a lover's sigh.

"The wind," my mother said, "is trying to make up its mind whether to be a breeze or a hurricane."

"Like the big wind," Grandfather Stefanos said, "in . . . in . . ." He paused, trying to remember the date.

"The day after Easter in nineteen hundred and fifty-six," I said to help him out.

"Fifty-eight," my sister Daphne said, more to put me down than to help Grandfather remember.

"It was the year fifty-nine," he said and hobbled out on the porch, repeating the date. He went down the steps and stood among the palmettos and stared up at the sultry clouds that had turned from white to blue-gray just while we were sitting there at the table.

My grandfather was short and thick through and had a round head. His hair was cut close and looked velvety, like an animal's pelt. When he was young and came to Florida his name was Stefanos Papadimitrios. But when he was married his wife didn't like the long name, so to please her he cut off part of it and became plain Stefan Dimitrios.

Once each year, however, when the bishop came on Christ's Baptism Day to bless the sponge fleet, when everything was quiet, even the gulls, Grandfather would take a prominent place on the wharf.

Then he would give a short speech, with gestures he had practiced in front of the mirror at home. Thumping himself on the chest, he would proudly say, "I am Stefanos Papadimitrios from Kalymnos in Greece. I am the first man, almost, to dive for sponge in the United States of America."

Grandfather Stefanos hobbled back into the house and sat down but didn't eat. "Twelve boats sank in that wind. But not my *Cybele*. She went up the river and over the wharf," he said, "and up Dodecanese Street. With me, Stefanos, hanging onto the rudder . . ."

We had heard the hurricane story before. My sister, Daphne, was watching TV while she ate, while she waited for her date to come. My mother kept glancing out the window at the bending trees. Far beyond were the waters of the Gulf, where my father had gone to dive for sponge.

Mile after mile on the whole vast floor of the Gulf of Mexico they spawn, the best sponges in the deepest water. There are two banks in the Gulf — the Mexico Bank, which runs out from the coast where the water is seventy feet deep, from the Florida Keys to Cape San Blas, and the Middle Ground Bank, far offshore. It is safer to dive for sponge on the Mexican Bank, but my father had gone to the waters of the open Gulf. He would be gone for two weeks.

Sometimes when Grandfather told his story, he said that below him there in the singing waters he saw a mermaid basking on a rock and a school of manatee waiting upon her. Other times it was Poseidon himself whom he saw.

"What did you see when you were sailing along Dodecanese Street, peering down from the deck of *Cybele?*" I asked to urge him on.

But Grandfather didn't answer. He was thinking about the wind.

Over her shoulder, Daphne watched a fashion show in Tampa, where models were walking around in a restaurant, showing off bathing suits. "Last time," she said, "it was the fabled island of Atlantis and treasure ships that Grandfather saw."

Grandfather was not pleased to be reminded that he often varied his tales about the day he sailed up Dodecanese Street in the hurricane.

"Not Atlantis," he said. "I saw Daphne Dimitrios sitting on a red motorcycle, fixing her hair."

My mother got up and went to the front window. She was a tall woman and thin, thin as my father and taller, though he would never admit it, with wide shoulders, almost as wide as mine.

"Athena," Grandfather Stefanos said, "calm your fears. The wind is a kitten that purrs, not a tiger."

Gusts were playing around on the roof, lifting the shingles and letting them flap back. In the yard, stiff Spanish bayonet was bending to the gusts. Mother sat down again, covered her ears, and stared out the window. Far off now, through the dark haze, I could see the Anclote light.

Flashes from the lighthouse lit up the room every few minutes and made Mother look even paler than she was.

Grandfather had been talking in English, but now, as he saw how disturbed she was, he began to speak in Greek.

"Your husband Elias," he said, "is a man acquainted with storms. He has fished the Gulf for most of his life. I took him there when he was ten, on his tenth birthday. Thirty years ago. Elias has learned much since then. One of the things he has learned is to come in out of a hurricane."

He glanced at the pictures of my father that hung on the wall above the TV set. Mother had arranged them in a horseshoe. Starting at the bottom on the left side was my father on the day my grandfather took him out to the Gulf and showed him how to dive for sponge.

There were a dozen pictures of him, and at the very top he stood on the deck of his ship in diving gear, with me at his side, holding his diving helmet. The photographs had been colored by Mother's hand and were not quite true in color. His eyes, for instance, were not the midnight black she had painted them but a dark shade of gray, as gray as mine.

I was very proud of my father. Like the other captains of our sponge boats, he was a hero in the town of Tarpon

4

Springs. When he walked up Dodecanese Street people admired him. They knew that he went far out in the dark waters of the Gulf and calmly faced the dangers of the sea. Sometimes I imagined myself as his son, diving beside him in the deep waters of the Gulf.

The siren at the firehouse in Tarpon announced the hour of seven, a bleating, sheeplike sound that made you grit your teeth. None of us in Bayou liked it, but we had little to say about what went on in the Tarpon firehouse — or, for that matter, over in Tarpon itself. In the old days, when half the Greeks in Greece it seemed came to Tarpon Springs to live, we had everything to say.

The firehouse siren no sooner died away than a car came nosing up the street and parked in front of our house. The motor kept running.

I glanced out the window. Hibiscus bushes and palm trees were in the way. I had never seen the car before. All I could see of the driver was a lot of black hair, yet I knew who it was. So did Daphne, but she took her time finishing the food on her plate and ten minutes getting out the door.

It was past seven o'clock on a Saturday night, but Grandfather must have thought that she was hurrying back to work at the curio store. "Sell lots of sponges," he called out.

I watched her run across the lawn, which needed mowing, light-footed in her party dress, her unbound hair flying in the wind. She looked like the nymph Daphne, her namesake, fleeing through green meadows, pursued by the god Apollo. Only she was not fleeing and her pursuer was not Apollo, but Spyros Stavaronas.

5

Mother turned the TV dial to the Tampa station that was tracking the storm. Grandfather Stefanos went to the window and watched my sister get into the car. He must have caught a glimpse of the driver.

Speaking again in Greek, he said, "This young man who sits impolitely in the car and won't come to the door, who is this one?"

"Spyros Stavaronas," I said.

"And this one's father, which is he? The one who sells curios or the bald one who runs the café where they serve stomachaches with the pizza? Or the one who freezes shrimp and sends them away wrapped up in fancy cartons that weigh less than they're supposed to weigh?"

"He belongs to the Stavaronas who packs the shrimp," I said.

"Herakles, the son of the murderer?"

"Herakles Stavaronas," my mother broke in.

There was a horrible story in our town concerning Herakles Stavaronas. Some people believed that he was the son of a murderer and some did not. My grandfather was one of the believers.

It was supposed to have happened during the war, when the Nazis invaded Greece and rounded up all the Jews they could find. A Greek merchant made a contract to help them find Jews. He arranged that all the Jews would come to his village and he would put them in fishing boats and take them over to Turkey for money — all the money they had. The merchant told the Jewish men that they would have to go first, before their women and children.

So he separated the families and took the women and children to a cove down on the shore. Then he came back and told the men that their families were safe. The men were put in the boats, and when they were away from the shore Nazis, disguised as fishermen, fell upon them and killed every one of them and threw their bodies into the sea. Then the merchant went back to the cove where he had left the women and children, and while they were asleep he killed most of them with his knife.

Grandfather Stefanos had heard this story and he swore that the merchant who killed all the Jews was Fanorio Stavaronas, the grandfather of Spyros Stavaronas.

"I have never heard of this young man," Grandfather said. "In the shop where Daphne sells stuffed baby alligators, the alligators have black shoe-button eyes that remind me of those that belonged to Fanorio Stavaronas. Does his grandson Spyros have the same shoe-button eyes?"

Neither my mother nor I answered him.

"You must know this Spyros," Grandfather said to me. "You must have gone to school with him."

"He graduated from high school a long time ago," I said. "I used to see him when I was growing up. At church on Sundays and feast days. He was an altar boy. I don't remember that he had shoe-button eyes, but perhaps he did. I haven't seen him for years. He's been to college and off fishing for shrimp."

The weatherman in Tampa announced that the wind was now a hurricane — he called it Clarence — and that it was veering east by southeast to the south of Anclote Key.

"She'll miss us," Grandfather said.

Mother was gazing through the window at the tumbling clouds, thinking of my father, hundreds of miles away in the open Gulf.

Grandfather said, "He's safe out there. Quit worrying. And you, Aliki, get yourself calm. You'll be late for the dance."

I hesitated to leave.

"Let us go," said my mother.

We went together, stopping for my friend Angeliki on the way. At the church, my mother went inside and swept up all the dust in front of the altar and put it in a cloth bag. Then we walked down to the river and Mother threw the dust in. The river, she believed, would take the dust away to the sea and still its turbulent waters.

Angeliki and I decided that just for fun we would wear long dresses to the dance instead of our jeans, so I went back with Mother to change my clothes.

When we got home, Grandfather Stefanos was walking back and forth on the porch. He was not really walking. It was more of a little dance, a hitching, stiff-jointed shuffle that came from the time he was diving in the Gulf and came up too fast from the deep water. When a diver does that he often dies, because air bubbles get into his blood. If he does not die, then he has "the bends" for the rest of his life.

Grandfather pointed with his cane toward the Gulf, where black clouds were tumbling about. "The wind sees holy dust in the Anclote River," he said, speaking solemnly in his English.

2

On Saturday nights in the summer our church held a community dance. Everyone was invited and admission was only a dollar, so there was always a crowd, not only townspeople but also tourists. Usually there were more tourists than townspeople because Tarpon was known as the sponge capital of the world, and tourists came to see how we Greeks lived and dressed and how we fished for sponge in the warm waters of the Gulf.

My friend Angeliki and I went to the dances together after she broke up with her boyfriend and I broke up with mine. It was all right going single because we could count on my sister to find us partners. She was the most beautiful girl in Tarpon and the most popular. People said that her namesake Daphne, the forest nymph who broke Apollo's heart, surely must have looked like my sister.

Angeliki and I got to the dance late, after it had started. The older people were doing a nisiotiko, a happy, lilting, hand-holding dance, and the young crowd was standing around the punch bowls, drinking purple punch and waiting for the music to change. They were talking about the hurricane, which now had veered southward and struck the coast at Tampa, twenty-five miles away.

The evening star showed low in the sky. Paper lanterns were glowing in the trees. Hot gusts of air that smelled of the sea blew through the garden. Everyone was excited that the hurricane had passed us by.

When the hand-holding dance was over and all the bouzoukia and violins started a wild beat I danced with one of Daphne's suitors, who spent most of the time trying to find out things about her that were none of his business, like did she go with Nick Valos on Sunday night to see the Woody Allen picture at the Bijou Theater.

But he did teach me a new dance when the rock music began, one where you hold your hands up in front of you, palms out, then close your fingers fast five times, then pump your arms close to your body like a rooster crowing, then crouch low to the floor and wiggle your bottom back and forth rapidly six times, then straighten up, take ten steps, ten breaths, and do it all over again. I don't know what it was called but it was fun, if you dance it with a crowd and the mandolins and zithers are cackling like a barnyard full of chickens.

While I was dancing, I saw Spyros Stavaronas and my sister standing among the trees. Pale lantern light fell on them, turning his hair to shining metal, hers to golden honey. When the music stopped and I was having a glass of the purple punch I saw him dodging through the crowd, brushing people aside, coming in my direction. Then he was right in front of me. Then we were face to face and he was asking for a dance.

He had changed so much that for a moment I wasn't sure he was Spyros Stavaronas. He was no longer the shy altar boy I remembered, the image fixed in my mind of a skinny youth dressed in an angel's robes, with a fat nose and big feet and an odd way of bouncing up on his heels when he walked down the aisle.

There's a marble statue in the library in Tarpon, on the counter in front of you, just as you walk through the door, of the Greek god Poseidon, whose realm was the sea. All his features are perfect — the rounded chin, the straight nose, the broad forehead, the cap of tightly curled hair. That was the way Spyros looked — exactly like the god Poseidon — as he stood there and asked me to dance. Except that the statue was white and Spyros Stavaronas was dark from the sun and wind.

Lights turned in slow circles, casting rainbow shadows over his face as he looked at me, waiting for an answer. My hand began to tremble, and I put the drink down before it spilled.

I don't know how I found the courage to speak, to say a word. Nor why I ever said what I did.

"I hurt my ankle while I was dancing that funny step," I said. "I think it's sprained." And no sooner were the words out than I wanted desperately to take them back.

Spyros Stavaronas glanced down at my ankle. With my long dress, the tips of my slippers were all he could see.

"I'm sorry," he said. And he must have believed me because he added, "Now you can't compete in the festival. Daphne told me that you were going to swim in the big race. What a disappointment! But don't cry, there'll be another one next summer. And the next. You're just a kid yet." He turned his head to one side and admired my dress. "How beautiful," he said.

Spyros danced the next dance with my sister while I stood in the shadows and bit my tongue and watched him turn her away with a careless shrug, then draw her back to him as if he meant to hold her forever.

The swim festival for the Blue Dolphin Trophy, given by the governor of the state, was held the following day. By then I had overcome my embarrassment at lying to Spyros Stavaronas about my ankle, or some of it, at least.

The race was a half-mile swim up the river, against the current. I was in the lead by a full two lengths, moving comfortably at twenty strokes a minute. All but the last ten of the final hundred yards of the swim was under water.

I reached the hundred-yard marker and went down three feet, where the current ran slower than it did on the surface. The pace was slower here, but I was in a world I was used to. Since the first time I dove with my father at Anclote Key I had loved it. It was a realm of my own, where my body seemed weightless and my thoughts were free. I swam smoothly now and with confidence.

Through the clear water I saw the ten-yard marker. I kicked back to the surface and set off for the finish line, now five lengths ahead of the nearest swimmer. It was then that I made the mistake.

One of the big white shrimpers was moored at the finish line. Flags flew from her mast and on the deck a band was playing the Greek anthem. The three judges were gathered in the bow. I saw all this — the ship, the band, the flags, the three judges — in a quick second. Then I saw Spyros Stavaronas standing at the rail. The sun shone on his braided cap and on the gold buttons of his jacket. He looked down at me and raised his hand to cheer me on.

I don't know what happened. It could have been that I quit breathing or lost sight of the finish line or just floundered. Whatever happened, the girl I had led for all but two yards of the race slipped past me.

There was a gala reception afterward. The bouzoukia band played, the governor gave a speech, and I was presented with a bronze medal for coming in second. The medal had the figure of a dolphin on it and a blank place for my name. I looked for Spyros Stavaronas everywhere among the crowd, but he was not there.

The band played all afternoon and people danced on the wharf. Still he did not come. At dusk I saw the big shrimper, *Sweet Melina,* leave the dock across the river where she was moored and head downriver for the Gulf. As she disappeared around the bend, as my heart sank, I caught one brief glimpse of Spyros Stavaronas standing on the bridge in his gold-buttoned jacket, his face so dark beneath his braided cap.

# 3

At noon a week later, the sloop *Cybele* came slowly up the river, her two-cylinder engine missing fire. Usually my father sailed her in to save fuel. I ran down to the wharf and caught the mooring line as Steve Parsons tossed it ashore. The boat had come in a week early, which alarmed me.

Parsons, who manned the pump and lifeline, called from the deck, "Captain Elias is sick. He's in the cabin."

I hurried up the ladder and went below. My father lay on the floor, cramped between the two bunks. He looked up but had trouble focusing his eyes and did not recognize me until I spoke. He was still in his diving suit, everything except the helmet.

"What's wrong, Father?" I asked.

He closed his eyes and did not answer.

I glanced at Steve Parsons. "The bends?" I asked him, fearing that my father had suffered the most dreaded of all the injuries that can befall a diver.

Parsons started to speak. I stopped him. "Run and call an ambulance. Run fast!"

My father stirred himself. "Home," he said distinctly.

I did not argue with him. He had a terrible fear of doctors and hospitals.

He was not much bigger than I, but we had a hard time getting him down the ladder. I wanted to go for our car and take him home that way.

"I'll walk," he said. "It is safer than when you drive."

The three of us — Parsons and Tasso, the other member of the crew, and I — got him out of his diving suit and we all started up the hill. By now Mother was running toward us, her black hair streaming. We met her halfway up the path.

"What's wrong?" she said, the same fear in her voice that all the wives and mothers had when their men came home sick from the deep waters of the Gulf.

"Nothing," Father said. "What do we have for supper?" His speech was slurred.

After that he said nothing until the next morning, when he spoke a few words that nobody understood to the doctor Mother had called twice in the night.

Nikos Samios, the doctor, said, "Captain Elias, I am taking you to the hospital. You are a sick man. I think you are suffering from the bends, but I need tests to be certain."

"You do not need tests," Father said. "I am certain already."

"Of what?"

15

"Of the bends."

"You have some of the symptoms but not all of them," Dr. Samios said. "I prefer to take you to the hospital."

Father shook his head, stared about the room, and said nothing.

The doctor sent me off to the drugstore for a prescription and a tank of oxygen. I raced to town to get them and raced back, getting stopped on the way for speeding. Then I went to look for Steve Parsons. I found him in the Lighthouse Café, drinking beer with Tasso.

Parsons pushed a chair toward me. "You're too young to drink," he said, "but how about a lemonade?"

I shook my head and stood while he drank his beer. "You were on the boat when the accident happened. What did happen?"

"Ask your father," Parsons said.

"He won't talk about it."

Parsons drank his beer and wiped his mouth on the blue and white handkerchief around his neck. "He's the one who knows."

"But you were on the boat. You were tending the lifeline and pump."

Parsons coughed. "You're not blaming me for what happened?"

"Not at all, Mr. Parsons."

It was possible that he had made a mistake, overlooked something, and was trying to cover his tracks. He might have let the air pressure run low or the air hose get fouled in the propeller. He had come to Tarpon Springs from the north and drifted around from one job to another until my father picked him up. In good times he would not have been hired.

Parsons was watching me in the frosted mirror that ran along the wall behind the bar. He was bald on the top but had big tufts of hair above his ears.

"What happened?" I asked him again.

The bartender drew a glass of beer, swiped the foam off with a stick, and slid it down the bar. The waiter brought it over to the table.

"Tell her," Tasso said.

"When I'm ready," Parsons said, taking a drink of his beer.

"It was near night," Tasso said, "and we were far out."

Parsons gave him a vicious look. "Who's telling this story, anyway?" he asked. "We were far out on the Middle Bank," he began. "He'd been down an hour or more at a hundred feet. I thought maybe he had lost track of time, so I gave him a signal on the lifeline. I got nothing back. But right after that, in less than five minutes, he was up on top."

"He came up the ladder and sat down," Tasso said. "He looked all right, but when I got his helmet off he was white, white like a shark's belly, and his eyes looked funny."

"Did he say anything?"

Parsons shook his head.

"What did you do?" I asked him.

"I'd heard of the bends, of course. And I thought that's what it was. I'd heard that the best thing was to send the diver back down to fifty feet or so and have him stay there for a while, then come up to thirty feet and stay there for a while, and then come up all the way to the top."

"We'd heard that," Tasso said. "But he wouldn't let us bolt the helmet back on. There was nothing to do but head for home."

"Captain Elias was quiet all the way," Parsons said. "Except once, he raised up and shouted a word. It sounded like Greek, like ALLA- ZOH-NEE-YA."

"Probably the Greek word *alazonia*."

"What does that mean?" Tasso asked.

"Arrogance."

"He shouted it clear and only once," Parsons said.

That was all I got out of the two men.

Father was asleep when I reached home, but later, in the middle of the night, he began to talk about sharks, fifteen or twenty leopard sharks that were pursuing him, not in the sea but on land, through a forest of tall red sponge.

After he quit talking about the sharks, he lay quiet. Then at dawn he roused himself and spoke one word in Greek. The word was again *alazonia*. I asked him what he meant, but he wouldn't answer.

The doctor came early in the morning, and as soon as he had taken my father's temperature he said that the family must prevail upon him to go to the hospital. We tried — all four of us — but Father answered by pulling the sheet over his face.

That night he was no better, so Grandfather, who from the beginning had wanted to use his remedy for all bad sickness, got it down from the attic, where my mother made him keep it.

The remedy was called *balsamo,* oil of mouse, and he made

it outside in the woodshed, then put it in the sun for a long time to cure, and then stored it in the attic. To make *balsamo* he caught baby mice, three of them, when they were still hairless and blind, and put them in a bottle of olive oil and set the bottle in the sun for at least a year. The longer they stayed in the sun, the better the remedy was.

He rubbed the *balsamo* on my father's chest, which was the place that seemed to pain him the most, but it didn't help. He got worse during the next two days. Then, peacefully, on the third day at dawn, speaking the Greek word for "arrogance," as Mother held his hands, as I prayed on my knees, he closed his eyes forever.

Through the window, kneeling there, I saw that the sky beyond Anclote Key was bright with bands of pink and amber. The first light shone on *Cybele* riding quietly on the river tide, and it came to me sadly that she would never go to sea again with Captain Elias at her helm.

**4**

From the cemetery that looked down on the Anclote River, we came home, and my mother gathered us in the parlor. It was a cloudless day with a seaborne wind and the sun streaming through the windows.

"We should talk about money," she said. "*Cybele* lies at the pier. Her captain is dead. She will sail no more. We have debts and no money to pay them."

Daphne said, "I can give five dollars a week out of my salary."

Daphne was not tight with money, only with things that money couldn't buy.

"And Aliki can get a job with the town. They're advertising for girls to work in the afternoons."

I had seen the ads. The Chamber of Commerce was hiring

couples to dress up in Greek costumes and walk the streets of
Tarpon for the amusement of tourists. The girls were to wear
many-colored skirts and sashes, embroidered vests and veils,
while their escorts wore short white skirts and leggings, red
vests and caps and shoes with the pompoms of the Evzones,
freedom fighters in the long war against the Turks.

"They're paying three dollars and seventy-five cents an
hour," Daphne said. "You have a good figure, Aliki. You'd
look good in that costume."

"No," I said, shivering at the thought of parading in the
streets and being gawked at by sightseers. "I'll find something
else, thank you."

Grandfather had said little since my father's death — a few
pinched words of greeting at breakfast. That was all. He sat
on the porch through the day, silently wrapped up in his own
thoughts. He was silent now, his eyes on the sun that was
sinking fast behind Anclote Key.

"*Cybele* is sound," said my mother. "She is worth money.
We will sell her and pay our debts and have something left.
Alexandra can find work. I can find work. We will make
out."

"Everyone will find work except me," Grandfather said
and fixed his gaze upon my mother. "I know what you are
thinking. You are thinking that Stefanos Papadimitrios is a
nuisance. You wish him to wander away somewhere and disappear. I know, I hear it in your voice. Disappear, old man!"

Mother was accustomed to his outbreaks. She shook her
head to shame him.

Grandfather was not ashamed. "The Indians who lived here in the old days were more kind," he said. "When a man grew old and useless, his son would slip up behind him and hit him on the head with a club and kill him."

My mother gave him a pitying look.

"It calls to mind a story," Grandfather went on, still unashamed, "that happened on an island near Kalymnos. The old grandfather must have been eighty-five. The family got so they didn't like taking care of him. The expense and trouble and everything. One day they got out the donkey and a basket with the old man's few things, and they started to get the donkey ready to send the old man away, off into the wild mountains to die. Well, the head of the family told his son, who was yet a boy, to make the blanket ready to put on the donkey's back for the old man to sit upon. The boy looked at the father. He looked at the old grandfather. Then he pulled out a knife and started to split the blanket in two pieces.

" 'Why are you splitting the good blanket?' the boy's father asked him.

" 'Well,' said the boy, 'I am going to put half the blanket on the donkey for the old man.'

" 'And why,' the father said to his son, 'why are you doing this?'

" 'I wish to save the other half of the blanket for you,' the son said. 'For the time I send you away on the donkey.' "

Grandfather glanced at my mother, waiting for her to ask what the father had done then. When she didn't ask, he said,

"The father wept, he was so ashamed, and the old man stayed on with the family until the day of his death."

Daphne said, "Grandfather, you made money when you stuffed the sheep for everyone. You used to stuff twelve or fifteen in a day."

Years ago, before he was stricken, Grandfather prepared sheep for all the housewives in Bayou. It happened for the big Easter celebration. A whole truckload of fat sheep would come down the road from Georgia and he would stuff them.

"You got five dollars for every sheep," Daphne said. "Sometimes more."

"And sometimes less," Grandfather grumbled. "Sometimes there was nothing. From friends, nothing."

Grandfather was an artist at stuffing sheep, and he always was in great demand from our housewives.

He would go from house to house, starting at dawn, and the woman would bring out her sheep. After it was killed and hung up, he would make a small cut in the hide near the hoof; then he put his lips tightly to the cut and blew hard. The hide would separate, and he would peel it off like a glove from a hand. Then he would get the carcass very clean and stuff it with pecans and rice moistened with a fine sauce made from olive oil, tomatoes, and a sweet thyme that comes from the mountains of Greece.

"That happened at Easter," Grandfather said. "Easter comes one time in the year. And besides, I can no longer blow hard. My lungs are too weak for the mighty blowing that's required."

Bored with all the depressing talk, Daphne got up and turned on the TV. Mother put a kettle of water on the stove to heat. Grandfather hobbled to the front window and stood looking down at *Cybele* as she rode on the river tide, held fast at her moorings.

"Stefanos Papadimitrios is not the man he was years ago on the island of Kalymnos," he said. "Now the bones are sticks. Now the heart jumps from a walk across the room. Now the eyes see double — what is there and what is not there." He smote himself on the forehead. "Stefanos Papadimitrios is a beached whale."

When no one spoke to contradict him except me, and then halfheartedly, he turned to face us. Suddenly he threw back his shoulder and raised his voice.

"The beached whale bestirs itself," he shouted. "To the astonishment of all, it comes to life. It breathes. It finds its way back to the sea."

My mother must have known something of what was in his mind, for at once she grew pale.

"Tomorrow," he said, "we start on *Cybele,* scrubbing decks, cleaning. In a week, she's ready to sail."

"With what? Who sails the ship?"

"Captain Papadimitrios sails the ship."

"Without a crew?"

"No, with Parsons and Tasso."

"Who dives?"

"No one. We will not dive. We will use the waterglass and the hook. I know from the old days good places where sponge grows in the shallows."

"There is little money hooking the shallows," Mother said. "And it is dangerous. Like diving."

"It is dangerous in these days even to breathe the air," Grandfather said. "To walk down the street is dangerous, too. To cross the street is to commit suicide."

"You can't go out to the sponge beds with two men," my mother said, "one of them old. And the price for sponge is the lowest in years. Wire sponge, which is all you will find in shallow water, is the lowest of all."

She was fending him off. She was certain of what was in his mind and what he would say next. I also knew.

"The ship is yours," she said. "For years you have promised to give it to your son. But you never did give it. It's yours and you can do with it as you wish. But you will not have Alexandra."

She went to the stove and made four cups of coffee. She placed three of them on the table and took a sip out of her cup, then went to where Grandfather was standing at the window.

"You can find another man somewhere. With Tasso and Steve Parsons you have enough crew to go," she said. "You will not have Alexandra. A girl was never meant to do this work."

Grandfather struck his forehead with the flat of his hand and swore. Then he said, "On the island of Kalymnos, where you were born, women dove for sponges. They were trained to dive. They went down with the men. You yourself were trained to dive. You did not dive because you got yourself married and came here to Florida in America."

"Yes, I was trained," my mother said, "and that is how I know that the diving is dangerous. I know also because my husband is dead from diving and you are crippled. I also know that on the island of Kalymnos, when the sponge fleet sailed for Africa, which it did every year, many of the women gathered on the shore. They were dressed in black and they wept, for they knew that no crew would ever return complete."

Grandfather went out on the porch. He slammed the door behind him and sat staring down at *Cybele*.

Daphne looked at herself in the mirror. She was dressed all in black and her white skin looked whiter than ever. She was beautiful. I guess there's just so much beauty to be divided up in a family. At least, it was so in our family.

"Do you suppose," she asked, "that Grandfather is getting soft in the head? I hope we don't have to put him in an institution. That would be very embarrassing, to have our grandfather in an institution and everyone talking."

"It's not such a bad idea," I said, surprising myself. "My going out with him. I've dived before with Father."

"When you were ten and you only splashed around in the shallow water," Mother said. "Would you rather go sponging than work at a good, clean, well-paid job and come home and have a decent meal instead of fish and lentils every night? Sleep in a comfortable bed instead of rolling around on a hard deck with the waves sloshing over you all night and the sun beating on you all day?"

"And our neighbors," Daphne said. "What will they think of it?"

"That Alexandra Dimitrios is crazy," I answered.
"A yo-yo," Daphne said.
Mother was silent.

**5**

*Cybele* was a chunky double-ender — that is, she was shaped fore and aft, back and front, like a canoe — and her lines were the lines of the boats that once had sailed the ancient waters of Greece. She was barely thirty feet in length, yet was the equal of stormy seas.

Grandfather took three weeks to get *Cybele* ready. He could have done so much sooner, but he had never liked the color my father had used on the boat. The underbody, which was blue, he changed to oxblood red. Her topsides he changed from gray to white. The rail he trimmed a brilliant orange. Her decks became buff and the houses, the ultramarine of the Gulf when the sun was bright.

He didn't do any of the painting himself except for the thwart at one side of the tiller. He had friends in Tarpon who came when he called on them — five men as old as he and all suffering from some form of the bends. The paint he got on credit from the hardware store.

"I want her to look like Jason's ship," he explained, "when Jason sailed among the Isles of Hellas."

Beached at the pier, she looked more like an ornament on a Christmas tree. But out in the changing waters of the Gulf she would look at home.

Word got around that Alexandra Dimitrios was to go sponging. It was something no woman in Tarpon Springs had ever done. To most of the women it was somewhat of a scandal. A sponging boat, among hardened men, was no place for a girl, they said, a girl still in high school. To their husbands I was brazen. To the sponge divers themselves, those who strutted proudly down the street and drank with a flourish their wine flavored by bitter resin, I was a threat. The dangers they endured in the dark waters of the Gulf would no longer be thought so dangerous if a woman would dare them. In their own eyes, in everyone's eyes, they would no longer be heroes.

Yet, on the morning we left, more than a dozen friends were on the pier to see us off with gifts of food and to wish us well.

"We go no farther than the shallows at Anclote Key," Grandfather said. "We'll be home by nightfall. Do not worry."

Gay handkerchiefs bound the hair of all the women, but my mother wore black, and when the boat left the pier and the women waved gaily, she crossed herself twice. My sister Daphne had to work and wasn't there.

The morning was hot and close as we chugged down the river. There were only the two of us.

"Today," Grandfather said, sitting with the tiller hooked under his arm and the palmettos along the bank baking in the sun, "we expose the new paint to the weather. Also we show you things about the sponges. Have patience. There is much to show. Remember it is old, this sponging. Recall when Christ said, 'I thirst,' the soldiers filled a sponge with vinegar and put it in his mouth. Your ancestors harvested sponge when Caesar ruled the world. What they knew is in your blood, Alexandra."

We went beyond the Anclote light, but not far. We fished the shallows in a cove that had not been visited in years, which Grandfather knew about. He showed me how to use the three-pronged fork and the sharp knife strapped at my waist.

He stood up with the tiller between his knees and lifted his shoulder as high as he could, which was not very high, and took in a great gulp of air, and another, gulp after gulp, until his chest was twice its usual size. Then he let out the air with a long *whoosh*.

"It is called swallowing the wind," he said. "And because it is important in diving with the sink stone, you must learn it."

I obeyed his command and filled my lungs with one breath.

"More," he said.

I took in a small gulp.

"More," he said.

I gulped again.

"For the first time it is good," Grandfather said. "You practice to stretch the lungs. Now we continue."

He handed me a stone that weighed most of twenty pounds. One end of a long rope was tied around it. The other end was fastened to the rail. I was already in my swimsuit, with a three-pronged, short-handled fork fastened to my belt and my goggles tightly fastened.

"How long can you hold your breath?" he asked me.

"I've timed myself three times," I said. "The best ever was two minutes and five seconds. That was before the big swim last June."

"We will do better. Before summer ends you will hold for three minutes. Some divers hold four minutes. Our cousin in Kalymnos — his name is Triandafilos — holds the breath five minutes. Then his face goes black and he falls over."

He took out his watch and clicked open the lid.

"I'll keep time," he said. "Two minutes and I'll pull the rope. Two times, hard. Gently now. Right side up and bend your knees and lean on the current. Sometimes it runs strong."

I took the wind twice and went over the side, clutching the basket and the heavy stone. The water was only nine or ten feet over my head. I struck bottom with a thump, buckling my knees, and straightened up to get a bearing. *Cybele* loomed above me, her red hull comfortably close. I could see Grandfather leaning over the rail, the sun glistening on his watch.

There was a good bed of sponge growing in a crevice, but

as I moved toward it, leaning forward as I was told to do, I saw a pair of eyes staring out at me. They were amber flecked with green and looked as big as saucers. It was a large grouper, half as big as I. Groupers are not friendly fish nor are they ferocious, but I decided to move on.

The water was as clear as air and Grandfather could watch me. On a hillock beyond the crevice I found a bed of sponge and lifted up seven, holding the stone against my chest and using the three-pronged fork.

My throat began to ache. The minnows swam up and began to nibble at my ears. I brushed them away but they came back like flies.

I let out some air through my nose and watched the bubbles shoot upward in a string. I was sure I had been down for more than two minutes. Suddenly the boat seemed far away. The current was dragging at me. I gritted my teeth and counted ten, then I dropped the stone and tumbled slowly to the surface.

Grandfather took the sack of sponges and I clambered over the rail. "We broke records. Two minutes and eighteen," he said. "Good. Next time we break a record too. Now we rest, huh, and inspect the sponges."

He turned the sack upside down and the seven dripping sponges fell out upon the deck. In the underwater light, with the sea currents playing around them, they had seemed alive. But here in the sunlight they looked like the severed heads of Nubian slaves, featureless and covered with a thin membrane that was shiny and pockmarked.

"Grass," Grandfather said. "Not the best, but they'll pay expenses."

He put them aside to dry out and I dove again along the same shallows, bringing up twelve more. The water was warm, but by nightfall my fingers had begun to wrinkle. When the Anclote light came on we headed for home, two hours away.

"Good. Fine," Grandfather said, setting his course on the lighthouse. "Tomorrow we go into deep water. No diving tomorrow. We will go with the waterglass and hook. You'll like tomorrow."

I nodded, too exhausted to speak, and went below and made myself a bed on a hard, wooden bunk and tried to sleep. The light from Anclote kept flashing into the cabin, first to port, then, as the boat shifted course in the choppy sea, to starboard. My legs were scratched and my lungs ached.

From the cabin roof hung my father's diving suit — the helmet with its three small windows, the heavy breastplate, the suit itself like long underwear except for the lead-shod boots. What I had done today had little to do with diving, with hardhat diving in the dark waters of the Gulf where the choice sponges lived. Would I ever learn? Would my father's suit ever fit me?

My doubts grew. We passed the Anclote lighthouse and its light no longer shone into the cabin. But my father's diving suit was still there, moving from side to side like a pendulum with the motion of the boat. It was a warning, a silent reminder of the diver's lot.

I got up and went on deck. Grandfather, holding the tiller between his knees, humming to himself, stopped humming and said, "Soon we'll go to the Gulf with waterglass. No danger with waterglass. One day out. One day work. One day back. Three days. But we'll say, 'Athena, gone four days.'"

"So she'll be pleased when we return a day early," I said.

One of the big sponge boats passed us, going seaward. Her riding lights shone on Grandfather's leathery face. He was smiling his crooked, fitful smile.

As the sponge boat set our boat to rocking, there came from the cabin the faint sounds of my father's lead-soled boots rubbing against the bulwarks, first on one side, then the other.

"Tomorrow I'd like to try the diving suit," I said. "Just to see if it fits."

"We'll make it fit. Sleeves too long now. Pants too long now. No matter. We'll pull up the sleeves and pants. Not tomorrow, though."

"When?"

"We will see."

Grandfather shifted the tiller to stop the boat from rocking.

"You had fear today?" he said.

"No," I answered.

Grandfather was silent.

"I am used to swimming underwater."

"Swimming," he said, "but not the walking. Not a playground, this sea business." He paused. "Perhaps a little fear?" he asked.

"Perhaps," I confessed. "It was when the bottom got stirred up and I looked over my head and couldn't find the boat."

"Good, a little fear is good, Alexandra. Your father had no fear. And I had no fear and have none at the moment. But it is best to have a little. The Nereids like to attack those who are arrogant and who are without fear. People speak of your father's death as mysterious, caused by this and that. But it was no mystery. I know the cause. The word *alazonia,* which he spoke as he was brought home from the Gulf, is proof that by his act of coming to the surface too soon — without fear and arrogantly — he had defied the laws of diving. He had angered the Nereids and they had taken revenge upon him."

Grandfather was talking about the fifty daughters of Nereus, the sea god, the son of Pontus and beautiful Gaea. In the past from time to time, when he was younger, he himself had encountered the Nereids. Sometimes it happened on land but usually on the sea. There was the time he had been diving since dawn. It was dusk. The deck was piled from rail to rail with wool sponges, the golden fleece, the finest of all sponges, a cargo worth a thousand dollars at auction.

He had told the story many times before. He told it again as we rounded the last head and came to the long, crooked channel before home.

"It is dark on the sea," he said, "but the sky is light off in the west, just like now. The music comes first. Lutes play, many lutes and voices. I see figures dancing. Beautiful girls dancing on the waves in dresses like white foam. They dance circles around the boat and sing. Beautiful girls, ten, perhaps there are more. The sun goes down and they go with the sun, down deep into the sea."

"They beckon to you," I said, as I always did when he told

this story of the Nereids, "and though the deck is piled with sponge, though the night is coming on, though you are tired and the crew is tired, and though they caution you, still you put on your diving suit and follow the dancing girls into the deep."

"Without fear I follow them," Grandfather said.

"Then you are brought up, unconscious and nearly dead."

"Dead. And since that day, half dead. The Nereids hate those who have no fear."

The first stars came out. The river bent south and we came within sight of our pier. On the hill above the pier, someone had built a small fire. Its light fell across the water and guided us home.

While Grandfather lashed the tiller, I tied the boat up bow and stern. Then I helped him ashore. My mother stalked down the hill, carrying a lantern. She raised a hand in greeting but said nothing. She climbed into the boat and glanced at the sponge we had taken, which was strung up to dry.

"You have a string of sponge that will bring next to nothing at auction," she said. "Barely enough to pay for the gasoline you have used this day."

Grandfather was leaning hard on his cane, blinking in the light of the lantern. "We only worked the shallows today," he said.

"And you will work the shallows tomorrow also," Mother said. "How can you work anywhere else until you have a crew? A girl not out of school and a crippled old man. This is madness, Stefanos Dimitrios."

"Stefanos Papadimitrios," he said, correcting her. It was the sign. He straightened himself and lifted his cane. "I will use the boat as it pleases me." He pointed into the night with his cane. "In the shallows or in the deep blue waters of the Gulf, as it suits me, for the boat belongs to Stefanos Papadimitrios."

"And remember this, old man. Alexandra belongs to me, to Athena Dimitrios. She is my daughter."

Grandfather planted his cane, thrusting his crippled body toward her. "And remember this, Athena. I go to the waters alone if necessary." He glanced at me. "If it is necessary."

Spongers were going out to the Gulf, to be ready for work at dawn. Our boat rocked at the pier, and again I heard my father's heavy boots thudding against the bulwarks.

Mother shone the lantern in my face. She must have seen my answer there, for without a word she left us and went back up the hill. When she came to the fire she stamped it out and went on, walking slowly.

## ❧ 6

We spent the next morning cleaning sponges and the next day at the auction selling them. There was barely enough money to pay for gasoline. With what was left over we bought supplies for our three-day voyage — two dozen eggs, a small sack of flour, a bag of Spanish beans, a bottle of olive oil, and three big rattlesnake melons.

Before dark we stored the supplies, filled the gasoline tank, washed down the deck, and ate supper. Mother had prepared my favorite dish. It is called *pastitsio me kima* and is made from macaroni and beef and eggs, cinnamon, pepper, chopped onions, butter, tomato paste, and lots and lots of Romano cheese. But it was not Grandfather's favorite and he only picked at his helping.

"I forgot," she said. "I know you don't like the *pastitsio,* but I made it for Alexandra."

"I have not liked it from the day I was six years old," Grandfather said.

"That was the day you found a rusty nail in the middle of your dish of *pastitsio*," Daphne said.

"And since," said Grandfather. "Always since."

"Do you wish me to cook you something else?" my mother said. "It will take only a minute or two and be no trouble." She paused, turning her head to one side and looked at him critically. "You will need strength," she added. "You are very thin. You forget that you're no longer twenty years old."

"I forget everything except that we work with the water-glass beyond the Anclote shallows and that we will be home in four days," Grandfather said and got up from the table.

My mother did not go to the pier with us. At the door she wished us well, and when Grandfather said that we would be back in four days, she said, "If you're not, I will speak a word to the Coast Guard and they will go searching for you."

As I went down the hill and looked back and saw her standing in the doorway, with the lights from the kitchen shining on her, my heart sank. Not until we left the pier and she was no longer in sight did I feel better.

There was a breeze blowing off the land, so we raised a sail to save gasoline. The night was dark and a strong current was running. While Grandfather steered, I stood in the bow as lookout. We had the river to ourselves until we came to the Anclote shoals. Then one of the big shrimpers loomed ahead of us.

She was coming in from the sea down the middle of the channel, her searchlight on, and running fast. All the Stavaronas shrimpers ran fast, beyond the five-mile-an-hour limit. Leaving port they were always in a hurry to reach the fishing grounds, and coming home they were anxious to discharge their cargo.

That afternoon, after I had left the auction and taken Grandfather back to the boat, I had gone to the Coast Guard station. I found a woman not much older than I, dressed in a blue uniform with silver stripes on the sleeves, standing at the window, looking out at the boats on the river. She turned as I came in, and from the faraway look in her eyes, I got the feeling that she would rather be out on the river than there in the office.

A card on her desk read: PETTY OFFICER MARY ROGERS.

"Miss Rogers," I said, "I am inquiring about the *Melina*."

She gave me an odd look out of eyes that were blue like frost. "What do you wish to know?"

"If the ship is still in Panama. My sister says it is."

The officer started to answer me, changed her mind, and took a ledger from the desk. She leafed through the pages and then, without really looking at them, said, "*Melina* has moved into Venezuelan waters."

I hesitated and at last got up the nerve to say, "Is Captain Spyros Stavaronas on the ship?"

The sergeant leafed through the ledger, again without really looking at it. "Spyros Stravaronas was the captain of the *Melina* when she left port. I assume he still is." Miss Rogers gave me another odd look. "The captain must be a charmer. You're the third girl this week to ask about him."

In my embarrassment I lied. "I am not asking about Captain Stavaronas. I have a friend in the ship's crew and I would like to know when he'll be home."

Petty Officer Rogers looked in a file on her desk, once more without really examining it. "The latest report has *Melina* home Tuesday of next week."

I thanked her and opened the door.

"Did you swim in the meet last month?" she asked me. "I seem to remember your face."

"My name is Alexandra Dimitrios," I said. "And I swam in the meet last month and came in second." I didn't tell her why I came in second.

"Dimitrios," the petty officer said. "Then you're the girl who's on *Cybele*. With your grandfather, the old man who has the bends, Stefan Dimitrios."

"Yes, I am."

"Well, *Cybele* has a good rating. She was inspected in January and rated sound. Except for the starboard riding light that had a broken glass. I assume it's fixed.

"Yes."

"And an air hose that should be replaced in another six months, anyway."

"My grandfather knows about it and will have it replaced. He has spoken about it."

I thanked her and was leaving when she said, "Do you know Captain Stavaronas?"

I was surprised, not by the question so much as by her tone, which I can't describe but which somehow gave me an uneasy feeling.

When I didn't answer, she leafed through the file on her

desk. Then she glanced up and gave me a quick, unfriendly look. "You've wasted my time," she said. "I have more important things to do than answer silly questions."

"I didn't mean to waste your time. I came to ask about —"

"Not a friend," she broke in. "You told me a lie. You came to ask about Captain Stavaronas. You've got a crush on him, like all the other dimwitted adolescents in town."

The officer's words suddenly came back to me as the ships passed us. "You've got a crush on him," she had said, "like all the other dimwitted adolescents in town." The ship crossed our bow, her searchlights playing on our deck. The officer might have lied to me. The ship could be the *Melina*. But I shielded my eyes and didn't look at her.

She left a trail of phosphorescence behind her and we followed it to the mouth of the river. Not once did I think of Spyros Stavaronas then nor when we anchored for the night in shoal waters, a mile beyond Anclote Reef.

7

At dawn Grandfather had me get the waterglass down from the cabin roof. There was a small platform just below the rail amidships, and he told me to kneel on it and use the contraption, which was simply a box with a glass at one end.

"Just hold tight to the box," he said, "and put your head into it and look at the sea bottom. After you get used to looking, when you can tell a sponge from a rock, I'll give you the hooking pole."

We were in the shallows, where the water was no deeper than twenty feet and clear. Lying stretched out on the platform with my face pressed against the waterglass and holding tightly to the box that held it, I could see the bottom, bunches of kelp swaying in the current and stretches of white sand. But nothing that looked like a sponge.

We moved on around a sandy spit and floated up so close to the shore that the mangroves cast shadows on the boat. There, through the bobbing waterglass, I caught sight of what looked to be a bed of finger sponge.

I reported the find to Grandfather, and he handed me a long pole with sharp teeth on the end, like a rake. "Measure the sponge first," he said. "By law, it must be the width of the teeth. Five inches. Then you use the hook and pry the sponge off the rock."

The glare of the water was blinding. The pole was at least thirty feet long and clumsy to handle against the shifting currents. In two hours with the hook I brought up only ten of the finger sponge. But Grandfather, sprawled at the tiller, was pleased. Each time I raked up a sponge he would say, "Good. Good. Again, we try."

By nightfall I had raked up from the bottom twenty-nine sponges — three of the flowerpot variety, three yellows, seven wire, and sixteen of the finger sponges. There are more than five thousand different kinds of sponge in the sea, but of this number, the twenty-nine I took that day were of the very poorest quality and value.

"Good," Grandfather said from his seat at the tiller. "Tomorrow we go south. More with the hook. I will teach you about the hook and the sponge. Big day, tomorrow."

The sun was sinking in a splash of changing colors — orange, then green, then amber and gold. I was glad to see it go. My face burned from the sun's reflection on what had been a windless day and a flat sea. My back ached. On my fingers were six fat blisters from the awkward hook pole.

Exhausted, I flung myself on the deck. As I closed my eyes, there ran through my thoughts the awful suspicion that Stefanos Dimitrios was reliving his past. Through me he was young again, a young man sailing a Grecian sea in a happier time.

"We will starve, all of us, at this rate," I said. "All day, and nothing to show for the work except a small pile of worthless sponge. Like the last time."

"We dive soon," he said. "We'll go soon for the good sponge — sheepswool and yellows. Now you must learn about sponges. Everything. I will teach you everything."

I said no more and he sat quietly musing, outlined against the western sky that was still pale from the last of the sun. As we drifted he held the tiller in one hand, peering out from under the brim of his huge straw hat. When he broke the silence he spoke in Greek, as he did when he was stirred by old memories.

"With all your school and all your American ways," he said, "you are still a girl of Kalymnos. Two thousand years are not lost in one lifetime, in the brief time of sixteen years. In the world of the many-celled animals," he said, "the sponge is the most primitive. Do you understand what 'primitive' and 'many-celled' mean?"

"Of course I do. I go to school. I am a junior in high school, remember?"

"That does not prove that you know what the words mean. To the contrary. Anyway, the sponge eats, grows, reproduces, and yet has no mouth, no internal organs, and no nervous system."

Night was falling fast. I reminded him that we should anchor.

"Good," he said. "We anchor here, now."

I let down our stern anchor and Grandfather pulled forward until it took hold on the bottom. Then he shut off the motor and I lowered the sail.

"Sponge have small pores in their outer skin," he said, "and the pores open into a system of tubes and canals, which are lined with whiplike hairs that lash the water constantly. These hairs cause the water to be drawn from the incoming canals and forced through the outgoing canals. From the water the tiny hairs trap plankton, which they feed upon. Are you familiar with plankton?"

I didn't bother to answer. A Coast Guard plane flew over less than a hundred feet above us, made a slow circle, and disappeared. When the noise faded and I could hear him again, Grandfather was still talking about the sponge and how it reproduces by making both eggs and sperm, then as a single cell drifts around until it finds a rock to fix upon for the rest of its life.

The night was close and hot. There was half an oil drum on the deck for cooking, but I did none. We sat and ate two of the three melons we had brought along. Small fish came up and swallowed the seeds we threw in the water. The Coast Guard plane came back again, its lights flashing against the cloudless sky, and flew off to the south, toward Tampa.

Grandfather went on talking. He was still talking when I fell asleep. The last thing I heard was that young sponge grow slowly until they are three, then they grow rapidly, and some of them grow bigger than wheelbarrows.

We hooked for sponges for two more days along the reef and at dusk on the third day sailed home. The next four days I spent on the pier with my mother, scraping away the tough dark skins, dousing what was left, the skeletons, in seawater, thumping those skeletons against the wood planking of the pier, and scraping them with a sharp knife to get rid of the sand and all the small creatures that lived in them.

Mother was pleased that we had come home a day sooner than she had looked for us. She cooked a big supper — *pastitsio me kima* for me, lamb souvlakia for Grandfather — and brought forth a bottle of sweet grape wine she had been saving for a festive occasion. But as we worked together on the pier, getting the sponge ready to sell, she was silent, speaking only to correct something I was doing wrong. She was not yet ready to relinquish me to the dangerous waters of the Gulf.

The next day, Grandfather sold all except two of the sponges at auction for a hundred and ninety dollars. The two, which were flowerpot sponge and extra-good specimens, I sold for twenty-three dollars to the curio shop where Daphne worked. When we got home at suppertime, the kitchen was dark and Daphne was sitting in front of the TV, eating potato chips out of a bag and drinking a Coke.

"Where's Mother?" I asked her, alarmed.

"She has a job now," Daphne said. "She's working after-noons down at the dock, selling tickets for the excursion boat. I got her the job this morning and she went down at noon."

47

The excursion boat took tourists out for an hour's trip on the river and gave them a demonstration of how men dived for sponge in the open sea.

"Why?" I blurted out before I thought. "Why did she do that?"

"Why?" Daphne said. "Are you stupid?"

"There was no need for Athena to take a job," Grandfather said. He pulled out the money we got at the auction and from the shop and laid it on the table. "Two hundred and thirteen dollars," he said.

Daphne glanced at the money. "That's for all that work? You were out for three days. You've been home for five days now, cleaning sponges. That figures out at less than twenty-seven dollars a day for both of you. Not to mention the expenses. Big deal!"

"We only practice," Grandfather said.

"We haven't really begun yet," I informed her. "I'm just learning."

"What have you learned so far?"

I started to tell her, but she was watching TV and wasn't listening. Then Mother came in. She'd had her hair done at the beauty parlor — the first time in years — and looked pretty. She had stopped at the deli on her way home and had an armful of little packages and buckets.

"We'll have a nice cold supper," she said.

While I was setting the table a horn honked in the street. Daphne put the last potato chip in her mouth and finished the Coke. At the door she asked, "When are you going out again?"

48

"Tomorrow we go," Grandfather said.

"Have fun," she said, and I heard her running down the path, light-footed like her namesake.

The cold supper was not nearly so good as Mother's own cooking, but neither Grandfather nor I said anything about it.

**8**

In the morning we took *Cybele* up the river and moored in front of the Lighthouse Café and waited for Steve Parsons and Tasso. They came as soon as the bar opened, but we stayed on the boat until they had had time to drink their first beer.

Grandfather had put up a sign on the wharf, asking for spongemen, the day he took over the boat. Prices were poor because the public was buying sponge made in factories out of chemicals. The synthetic sponge didn't last and didn't absorb water half as well as real sponge, but it was cheap and came in gay colors.

Spongemen worked on shares, not for wages. A share for a month's work in a poor market could be as low as two hundred dollars. Yet I think that this was not the reason the ads went unanswered. What sensible spongeman would choose to gamble his life with a crippled captain and a girl diver?

Steve Parsons, the floater, and half-bright Tasso were our only hope of gathering a crew.

"What's my share?" Steve Parsons asked as soon as we sat down beside him in the Lighthouse Café. "I got one share from Captain Elias. That's not enough. I need three."

Usually there were ten or twelve shares on a boat. Before the shares were divided, all the expenses of the trip were deducted from the sale of the sponges. Then, in a six-man crew, the owner-captain-diver got five shares, the diver two shares, the engineer one share, the lifeline tender one share, and the cook and deckhand one share each.

"How many in the crew?" Parsons asked.

"Four," Grandfather said. "The smaller the crew, the more shares we'll have," he reminded Parsons.

"Three shares," Tasso put in.

"I got one share before with Captain Elias, and he was a good diver." Parsons spoke to me, glancing at me in the glass behind the bar. "You are just starting, and your grandfather hasn't been out in the Gulf for fifty years. Even three shares is poor pickin's."

"And three for me," Tasso said, raising his mug of beer. The first knuckles on his thumb and fingers were tattooed with an animal's eyes. They looked like cat's eyes, slanted and yellow with black slits, and as he clutched his beer, the eyes seemed to open and close.

Grandfather got down from his stool and hobbled to the door. "Come," he said, "and see the new boat that will make you rich."

51

We all trooped to the door that opened onto the river and Grandfather pointed out *Cybele,* tied up at the wharf. In the bright sun, the boat in all its new colors glittered like a neon rainbow. The sight had no visible effect on Parsons, but Tasso blinked.

"Four shares and you divide them up as you wish," Grandfather said. "If you want more, go find yourself another boat."

Steve Parsons hesitated. He must have seen a chance to give himself three shares and Tasso one, for he said at once, "When do we sail?"

"Dawn tomorrow," Grandfather said, "if the weather holds. And we'll be out for two weeks, maybe three."

We left them at the Lighthouse Café and went to the hardware store, where Grandfather bought a belt for the diving suit, a smaller one that he thought would fit me better. It was the first time in all the times we had spent in the Gulf that I believed I was really going to wear my father's suit and dive in deep water.

Afterward we bought supplies for the trip, saving enough money to buy gasoline and oil. I carried everything out and stored it belowdeck.

There were two twenty-pound bags of Spanish beans, ten watermelons, a half-case of spaghetti, six bottles of Salonika peppers, tomatoes, cabbage, and red onions, a small wheel of feta goat cheese, dried milk, cloves, mace, sugar, salt, lemons, three dozen eggs, and for Grandfather only, a jug of bitter, black olives as big as prunes and a long braid of garlic.

Also for Grandfather, twelve cans of Norwegian sardines.

Imagine taking sardines out to the sea, where you can catch tons of fish in a single day!

We didn't leave at dawn, as Grandfather had planned. An engineer on the sponge boat *Calypso* had been killed in an explosion five days before. He had not been buried because the family was waiting for a brother to arrive from Greece, and it was a custom for a boat never to put to sea while a spongeman remained unburied.

At the last moment, when we did leave, Mother came down to the boat with a five-gallon crock of chopped lamb set down in heavy fat. It would keep well and give us a dozen good meals.

# ❧ 9

We set sail at dawn three days later on a fair land breeze, and late that afternoon in twenty feet of water I made the first dive in my father's suit. The suit fit me better than we had hoped, though it was a little long in the sleeves and bulky around the middle.

Before Tasso and Steve Parsons put the helmet over my head, Grandfather had me walk about the deck and climb down the boarding ladder.

My own weight was one hundred and twenty pounds. In the suit, holding the heavy copper helmet, I now weighed a little less than three hundred, so I staggered rather than walked. Then he gave me instructions about the lifeline, how to walk when I reached the bottom, and the proper way to control the flow of air into the helmet — a long list of dos and don'ts.

He said, for instance, "In the air hose there's a valve. Air goes through the hose and forces the valve to open. This is the air that fills the suit and cushions the terrible pressure from the outside. It is also the air you breathe."

"What if the valve doesn't work right?" I asked. "What if it shuts off the air and I can't breathe?"

"In that case," Grandfather said, "we will get a new diver."

Everyone laughed, everyone except me.

Tasso and Steve Parsons had come aboard red-eyed and sullen, but the sun had enlivened them somewhat. The compressor was running now, and the two hundred feet of air hose was neatly coiled on the deck. Together, the two men lifted the helmet and set it over my head.

"How do you feel?" Grandfather asked.

I couldn't hear him, but I read his lips after he had shouted three times. I shouted back, "Fine," though my knees were shaky.

Parsons turned up the bolts that fastened the helmet to the corselet and connected the air hose to the helmet. He guided my ponderous steps along the deck and onto the boarding ladder, and I went down one cautious step at a time until I was about three feet underwater.

I had four little windows — one in the top of the helmet, one on each side, and a large one in front. I glanced out of them one after another. Suddenly the woolen underwear I wore to keep from chafing began to feel like an iron glove, tight and hot and uncomfortable.

Sweat started to pour off my face and run down my chest. All the windows were now clouding over, but I could see

Tasso's hands gripping the lifeline, the yellow cat's eyes tattooed on his knuckles winking at me through the haze.

It was not too late to turn back, I decided.

I took a step back up the ladder. Then I saw my grandfather staring down at me. His face, magnified to twice its size by the water, filled the little window. I tried to think of an excuse for turning back. None came to me.

The pump started up. Air hissed softly from the hose and began to trickle down over my sweating chest. Grandfather's face grew larger; his thin lips tightened. In desperation I let go and floated away from the ladder.

I expected to go sailing straight down to the bottom, not twenty feet away. Instead, like a raft, I floated out from the boat and spreadeagled, my arms and legs sticking out stiff and straight as boards.

Steve Parsons pulled me in by the lifeline and got me back on the ladder. My feet in their leaden boots pointed downward. I had let too much air into the suit and it had ballooned on me. I adjusted the valve, let air out of the suit, and stepped off the ladder again.

This time I went down feet first, slowly, slowly, right side up.

I was less than halfway to the bottom when a searing pain, sharp as a needle, shot through both ears. I blinked back the tears that popped into my eyes and, remembering what Grandfather had told me, that all divers experienced this pain once the first seven or eight feet of water were passed, I yawned and jerked my head from side to side. The pain stopped, but my ears felt uncomfortable.

I was on the bottom in loose sand. The water was clear. I could see the boat above me and a chain of bubbles rising from the helmet.

Leaning forward, doubled over as I had been told to do, I took a dozen cautious steps, taking care not to disturb the loose sand. It rose up anyway in small gray clouds around my legs, and by chance I stepped on a stingray, which was the same gray color as the sand. At the end of his long tail he has a dark spike, which carries the same venom as a viper. When my foot pressed down on him, he instantly whipped up his ratlike tail and struck me a solid blow. Luckily, the spike did not go through my heavy boot.

Cautiously, I took a few more awkward steps, aware that I was more comfortable now, which meant that the air pressure was right. If it isn't right, as I was to learn, if you have too much air, you find yourself floating up to the surface. Too little, and the suit presses in on you like an iron claw.

I came to a small cavern overgrown with orange and red Gorogonia coral. Looking out at me from its midst was a lone inhabitant — from what I could see of it — a small hammerhead shark, an odd creature whose head is five or six times as wide as it is long and so flat that it might have been run through a wringer. To add to its monstrous shape, its eyes and nostrils sit at the outer ends of the misshapen head.

At the sight of me, the shark backed away into its shadowy den until all I could see of it were its eyes staring out, like the eyes of two creatures instead of just one.

The hammerhead gave me a start, and I didn't turn my back on it. I sidled away in another direction, though my father had told me that in all of the seventy-five years of sponge fishing in the shallow and deep waters of the Gulf, by thousands of sponge fishermen, not once had a diver been attacked by a shark — the hammerhead shark or the gray nurse shark, or the spotted leopard shark or even the great white shark, the one with the hundred sawteeth, who is as long as a boat.

Farther on, as I passed a second clump of coral, a gray tendril drifted across the window of my helmet. I brushed it off. But the tendril reached out and took hold of one of my fingers and pressed it in a gentle, friendly way. Then it withdrew, and I was looking into the amber eyes of a small octopus.

I carried a three-pronged fork and had a knife strapped to my thigh, but I made no attempt to take any of the sponge I came upon, and I saw several good ones. I was content just to slog under the drifting boat, glancing at bursts of coral and beds of sea anemone, somewhat like a window shopper strolling along a street, only that I was scared.

Not a minute passed that I didn't raise my head and stare out of the little front window to make sure that the bubbles were still there above me, pushing up from my helmet, racing each other to the surface. Nor a minute when I didn't hope that I would get the signal from the boat, telling me to end the dive.

The suit grew stifling hot. The air that came in through the hose began to smell stale and rubbery. Sound travels well underwater. I could hear waves breaking against the sides of the boat, and the sound made my ears feel uncomfortable.

Then, just as panic seized me, as I was about to flee to the surface the fastest way I could, the signal came — four sharp tugs on the lifeline.

I let air into the suit and rose a fathom and stayed there, grasping the lifeline, as I had been told to do. After my body had become used to the change in pressure, they pulled me up.

It was the happiest moment of my life when I sat down on the deck and they lifted the heavy helmet off my shoulders. I gazed around at the sea and the clouds and the blue sky as if I had never seen them before.

"You like it down there," Grandfather said, clapping his hands like a child. "Good. We'll send you down again after you rest. This time you will bring back fine sponge."

Tasso and Steve Parsons didn't clap their hands. They went about their tasks in silence and with sullen faces, wondering no doubt how they had gotten themselves mixed up with a crippled old man and a girl diver.

## ❧ 10

I dived twice more that afternoon, but to the disappointment of my grandfather and the crew, I brought back not a single sponge.

I was too busy with the air hose, trying to keep it from fouling on the sharp rocks, and with the air valve inside the helmet, which I could only adjust by sideways movements of my head. And always from minute to minute I felt I was a traveler in a strange world where perils lurked at every step.

It took another week before I brought up my first baskets of sponge, and these were of small value. We made three trips into the Gulf, but it was the middle of the summer before I began to feel at home in the sea. And it was a month later, on our fourth trip, that we struck the bonanza.

It came suddenly on a windy dawn. We were in water that

shoaled from ten fathoms at the eastern edge of Middle Bank. For almost a week we had been looking for a coral bar that Grandfather remembered from his early days as a diver. That is, he remembered where it was within a space of three square miles.

He now stood at the bow, peering down into the depths of the blue water. A wind had sprung up and the sea was choppy.

"We are near," he said, "but I do not see well through the chop. Bring the lead."

I brought the lead and the line it was attached to, soaped the bottom, and tossed it over the bow. We were under sail, moving at a speed of two knots or less. When the lead struck the bottom I pulled it in. Grandfather grabbed it from me.

"Bar-r-r," he sang out. "We have found the bar. And right where I thought it was all the time."

"You have a wonderful memory," I said, not mentioning that we had been sailing around searching for days.

The soaped end of the lead showed white shell dotted with pieces of pink coral.

Grandfather held it up. "Sponge," he said. "Acres of sponge right under our keel."

We took in sail and floated a buoy — attached to a spar with our green and yellow flag whipping at the top — to mark the place.

The surface of the sea was confused, but when I went to the bottom I had a good view in every direction for a hundred feet and more. Wool sponge, the fine variety that brought the best price at auction, grew everywhere on the sandy bar. As I went along with my sack, I felt as though I was picking cotton in a cotton field.

We were alone on the bar for three and a half days. I stayed down for as long as an hour at a time and made six dives each of the days. Working at night, we cleaned the sponge and strung it on lines and looped the lines on the mast. The deck was piled waist-high with uncleaned sponge.

At noon on the fourth day, I spotted a boat on the far horizon to the west of us. In a short time there were four boats, and they were headed in our direction.

They came upon us at dusk, as the wind died away, their riding lights shining over the water. They sailed within a quarter mile, all four of them, and anchored.

"Horning in," Steve Parsons said.

"Not fair," Tasso said. "We finding the sponge and they butting in."

If it were cod fishermen coming on each other or a couple of red snapper boats, things would be mean. There would be an argument and maybe a bloody fight.

Grandfather got out his binoculars. His eyesight was poor, so he gave them to me. I read the name of one of the boats.

"*Marjorie K,*" I said. "I can't see the other names."

"She's not from Tarpon," Grandfather said. "The name is not Greek. They must have come from the south somewhere."

I kept the binoculars on the boats. After a while two of them turned with the current and I read the names, *Kalymnos Girl* and *Nicola Sacharides.*

"Greek names," Grandfather said.

"Greek or whatever," Steve Parsons said, "they're aiming to take the food out of our mouths."

He disappeared and I heard him rummaging around in the cabin. He came back with a gun in his hand.

"What do you do with the gun?" Grandfather asked.

"Use it," Parsons said. "And it's a good one. Eight shot, Nambu automatic. Seven sixty-five."

"Japanese," Tasso said.

"The Nambu you use on what?"

"On whoever gives us trouble," Parsons said, flourishing the gun in the direction of the boats.

"Spongers," Grandfather said. "Some are Greeks. Greeks are welcome. We talk, not fight. Put the gun away."

We heard their voices as they ate supper and afterward when they played zithers and sang songs of home. In the morning their divers were in the water soon after I went down for the first time.

I had a sack full of sponges and had just given the signal for Tasso to pull it up. I bent over almost double to walk against the current and took a careful step. Slowly, from behind a treelike grove of coral, a diver came toward me, trailing a chain of bubbles. He held a sack of sponges in one hand and an iron sponging fork in the other.

I stopped. Taken aback by his sudden appearance, I nudged the valve by accident, let more air into the suit than I needed, and rose from the bottom. I had a notion to keep going. Then the diver raised his fork and waved it in an awkward greeting.

I let air out of the suit and went down again. The diver

came up to me, taking one heavy step at a time, and put a hand around my waist and held on. Then he put the front window of his helmet against mine — I could hear the two glasses scraping against each other — and spoke my name.

Our faces were only six inches apart.

"My name is Fundis," he said, "Johnny Fundis. *The* Johnny Fundis."

"I've never heard of you before," I said.

"You don't get around very much," Johnny Fundis said. "The name is known from the Keys to San Blas and beyond."

I couldn't make out what he looked like through all of the glass between us, but he sounded young and smart-alecky.

"I came over to ask you for the next dance," he said.

We were floating around in the current like two giant sea cucumbers. Two black and gold angelfish watched us, coming close, then backing away.

"I have the next dance with Poseidon," I said. Then I let half the air out of my suit — a silly thing to do — broke loose from his hand, and shot to the surface in a flurry of bubbles. I said nothing to Grandfather about this encounter or about coming up too fast.

**11**

There was a full moon that night. As it came up, we were
sitting around the fire that was burning in the oil drum we
used for a stove. We had finished the last of the lamb stew my
mother had put down for us when a shrimper came out of
the west along the track the moon was making on the sea.

*Cybele* was showing a riding light, and the other boats also
had lights at their masts. But the shrimper came straight toward us at full speed, tossing the sea up from her bow.

Twice during the day, while I was on deck between dives,
I had seen a shrimper trawling at right angles from us at a
distance of three or four miles. Once I had seen it nearer, not
more than a mile away.

The big shrimper was close upon us now, and I thought for
a moment that she meant to run us down.

A searchlight flashed on from her bow, a wide blue beam

that flooded us with light. Then the ship turned in a tight circle, reversed her engines, and came to a sudden stop in a fountain of spray. It reminded me of the times I used to go scooting along on my new ball-bearing skates right at somebody and then, just as I was about to run them down, skid to a screeching halt. Those were the days when I was young.

Waves spread out from the shrimper, big ones that rocked our boat and upset what was left of the lamb stew.

The searchlight swept across the spongers, one after the other, and came to rest upon us, turning all our faces a ghastly blue. The light swept away in a slow arc and finally pointed at the rising moon.

Then the light went dark and a burst of music floated across the water, the Athenian "Moon Song," played by zithers and bouzoukia.

The men from the sponge boats joined in the song, but there was not a sound from our boat. Steve Parsons and Tasso didn't know the song. Suspicious that the ship was one of Stavaronas' shrimpers, my grandfather sat silent and stiff-lipped.

There was a pause as the music ended, then a voice came across the water, speaking through a bullhorn. Even through the distance and the tinny roar of the horn I recognized it at once. It was the voice of Spyros Stavaronas.

"To you, Alexandra Dimitrios, and your grandfather Stefanos Papadimitrios, and to all your shipmates," he said, "and to all the men in the boats of the sponge fleet, congratulations on a rich harvest. Throughout the day I have seen you cover the decks, fill the holds, drape the masts with the finest sponge. I rejoice with you. Let's celebrate good fortune aboard my *Melina*. I'll send a launch. We'll have food and wine. We'll sing and dance all night. Come, friends. And Stefanos Papadimitrios, forget the past. Tonight we forget and celebrate. We will play the Black Chicken's Egg Dance."

The horn went silent and a motor started up, and I saw a launch head for the sponge boats. Steve Parsons jumped to his feet. Tasso went to the cabin and came back with his flashlight.

"We celebrate here," Grandfather said. "We celebrate now with our own good food and good company. We do not need Spyros Stavaronas to tell us how to celebrate."

"Great," Steve Parsons said, taking out his comb and arranging the tufts of hair over his ears. "We're on our way!"

"Great," Tasso shouted, waving his flashlight.

I was too excited to say anything. I went down to the cabin and found a clean pair of jeans and a shirt. The shirt was under a pile of sponge, wrinkled and smelling strongly of the sea. I shook it out and put it on. There was no mirror on the boat and no light in the cabin. As I brushed my hair, I felt my heart beating hard, not in my chest but in my throat.

The launch was unloading men from the sponge boats when I went back on deck. I watched them climb up the ladder and the launch leave the ship and head for us.

"You're not going." Grandfather said.

"It's rude not to go when we're invited," I said.

Grandfather got up and limped along the deck and came back.

"It's not as though we have a good excuse," I said.

67

"We don't need an excuse," Grandfather said.

Tasso was flashing his light on the launch that was coming toward us, throwing up spray.

"Why should Stavaronas get so friendly all of a sudden?" Grandfather asked. "It makes me suspicious. He must want something."

Steve Parsons went down to the cabin and came back with his gun shoved into the top of his trousers. He had on a Hawaiian shirt and it was pulled down over the gun, but you still could see the bulge. Grandfather said nothing about the gun.

The launch slid up to our stern.

I knew that Grandfather would never permit me to board the *Melina* unless he was there. It was all right for me to dive ten fathoms in the Gulf's deep waters but not to set foot alone and unprotected on the deck of a Stavaronas ship. Without another word I jumped into the launch. Imploring the heavens above, Grandfather scrambled in beside me.

The ship's big stabilizers were out on both sides and she rode steady in the waves. Lights shone at all her ports, and her decks were bathed in moonlight. For a brief moment she was a fairy ship on a fairy sea and I was a princess sailing to meet her adoring prince. Then everything changed. A flood of memories swept over me.

I remembered Spyros coming gaily across the dance floor while colored lights cast rainbow shadows around him, and me with a cup of purple punch in my hand as he asked me to dance, saying that I had sprained my ankle as I put the drink down before I spilled it. I remembered the race I lost because

I glanced up at the wrong time and saw him standing at the rail of the ship, looking down at me.

Spyros Stavaronas was looking at me now. He stood at the head of the ladder in his captain's uniform, his hair glistening like black metal in the moonlight — the sea god Poseidon surveying his watery kingdom!

"Welcome, Alexandra Dimitrios," he shouted in Poseidon's voice. "But be careful when you climb the ladder. Don't sprain your ankle again."

He laughed and waited for me to answer. I couldn't think of anything to say so I laughed, too, an embarrassed laugh that must have died before it ever reached his ears.

Grandfather couldn't climb the ladder, so the crew let down a net that they used to unload shrimp and we managed to get him into it.

The ship's ladder seemed to have a hundred steps and it pitched with the roll of the waves, but I went up hand over hand like a true sailor and, showing off, bounded on deck with a smile. But my heart was beating madly.

Spyros was there to greet me. He took my hand and led me to the afterdeck, where a place had been cleared off among the nets and chafing gear. A table covered with a red cloth sat in the center of the deck, with a great bowl of shrimp smothered in ice and around it mounds of tropical fruit and jugs of wine.

The musicians in the crew performed on their zithers and everyone danced arm-in-arm. Even Grandfather, after he had downed two drinks of the wine, got up and tried a few steps on his trembling legs.

Then Spyros and the young man I had encountered at ten fathoms in the diving suit danced the zeybekiko. They leaped out on the deck together. The searchlight focused on them. Puffing a cigarette, Spyros squatted and the young man pirouetted and pranced around him, clapping his hands. Then they changed places, the young man bent down, and Spyros did the prancing. It is an ancient war dance and is supposed to show an eagle swooping back and forth above its prey.

Spyros was very attentive. He ladled out a huge plate of shrimp for me that were as big as my fist.

"Fresh," he said. "Caught this morning."

The shrimp still had their heads and feelers, six eyes and fifty legs. They looked alive. I pondered as I held one by the tail, its beady eyes gazing at me, about what to do with it. I had never seen a shrimp so large.

"This way," Spyros instructed me. "You can't be squeamish about these monsters."

He grasped the one I was dangling and pulled off its head with one swift, twisting jerk as if it were the head of an enemy. Then he poured me a small drink of brandy. I took one sip and would have spat it out on the deck had he not been watching to see just how grown up I was. My sister Daphne would have drunk it, I felt certain, without a tremor to show her sophistication, though it burned her insides all the way down. And Daphne Dimitrios would not have hesitated a second to twist off the shrimp's head. She would say, "So what," even if it were alive.

"You and Daphne aren't much alike," Spyros said. "I wouldn't know you were sisters unless somebody told me."

The flood of silver moonlight seemed to turn him to marble. He was more the sea god Poseidon than ever.

"You don't look anything alike and you don't act alike," he said.

"Should we?" I managed to say.

"No, but I wonder how a girl who dives in the waters of the Middle Bank, a girl who does a man's job, who fills a boat until sponge hangs from the mast and over the sides, stern, and bow, can be so shy. Your sister, who works in a curio store selling sponge and knickknacks, isn't. I wonder about it."

How exciting, I thought, that he ever took the time to wonder. But when? Was it often or sometimes? And why? Why did he bother to wonder about me at all? I didn't find out that night.

While we stood there beside the table festooned with food and bottles of wine, a plane flew over the ship. It came swooping out of the north, circled the ship twice, and blinked its lights in greeting.

"Coast Guard," Spyros said. "They're checking on smugglers. There are a lot of them operating now. Heroin."

The plane was flying toward the Florida coast, its lights flashing, when one of the crew came to say that the plane was making a routine call on the phone and did Spyros want to answer.

As soon as he had excused himself, I tossed my brandy into the sea. Right after that, Johnny Fundis, whom I had encountered down in the coral bushes, came around to give me a hearty slap on the shoulder. He was shorter than I but wore high-heeled cowboy boots to make himself look taller. He had long sideburns that came down to a point. He turned out to be a pest who touched you on the hand every sentence or two. I got rid of him by saying that my grandfather needed attention.

And truthfully, he did. He had consumed too many glasses of wine, and this with his trembling legs had rendered him helpless. After an hour of coaxing, we finally got him into the net and lowered him to the launch and took him to the boat, and I put him to bed, happy as a lark.

The music grew louder. All the divers, all the ones who went down — and there were a dozen and more — danced the dance of the bends again and again. They laughed and shouted, mocking that terrible sickness of the deep. Only the divers danced it. Any of the hosemen or engineers or deckhands who dared to dance it would be struck down.

The party went on for hours, so loud that even the fish deep in the sea didn't sleep much that night.

# ❧ 12

Our boat was loaded to the gunwales. There was not a place anywhere — on the deck or the cabin roof or in the rigging — for another sponge. At noon, while Tasso and Steve Parsons were still asleep, we set sail for home.

The winds were contrary. It took us four days, sailing night and day, to reach Anclote Key. We pulled into our dock near midnight and found to our surprise a beacon fire burning on the hill and Mother waiting for us.

"Spyros Stavaronas," she said even before we hugged each other, "called two days ago to tell me that he had seen you on the Middle Bank and that you were on the way home. I looked for you yesterday. It was a thoughtful thing for him to do."

"Spyros Stavaronas loves the telephone," Grandfather said. It had taken most of the four-day voyage for him to get over the effects of the wine, and he had gotten around to blaming Spyros for his queasy stomach. "Stavaronas gave a party —"

"Spyros told me about the party," Mother said.

"He gave a party and most of the time he wasn't there. He was on the telephone, sending out calls. Talking, talking. As though he were the President of the United States."

"Anyway, it was nice of him to call me," Mother said. "I wasn't worried, but it was good to hear you were on your way home. And he told me about the sponge. I thought you'd come in with a good catch but not with two or three boat-loads."

In the moonlight you couldn't see the boat. It looked like a huge pyramid of sponge floating on the water.

"It's lucky we didn't sink," Grandfather said. "Your daughter is the best diver of all the divers on all the seas of this world, including those on the island of Kalymnos."

My mother fell silent. She tried to smile but only drew her lips together.

In the morning we went up the river and unloaded our cargo at the Sponge Exchange. It took us until dark to sort out the sponges by size, thread them twenty or twenty-five to a wreath, and arrange the wreaths in the courtyard so the buyers could inspect them on auction day.

Auctions were held on Tuesdays and Fridays. Since this was Thursday, Grandfather feared that everything might be stolen. He made himself a bed on one of the wreaths and spent the night with one eye open.

Word spread fast that Stefanos Dimitrios had come with a boatload of wools, the king of sponges, ninety percent of them round and soft as a lamb's fleece. On auction day the courtyard was crowded with buyers, more than had been seen for a long time.

The manager of the Sponge Exchange began collecting bids at eleven o'clock in the morning for several small batches of sponge, wires and yellows, that didn't belong to us. Then he collected bids for our sponge.

The exchange is owned by some three dozen packers and all of them were there, as well as a crowd of onlookers. The packers secretly write their names and the amount they wish to bid on slips of paper and hand them to the manager. The sponges go to the highest bidder if the owner is willing to sell them at that price.

The first bid he announced to the crowd was for twenty-one hundred dollars. The next two bids were for less, the next one for a few dollars more. The tenth bid was for twenty-six hundred dollars. This one brought a nod of the head from Grandfather. He was elated but did not wish to show it.

One of the packers was new to us. He kept strolling around our huge pile of sponges, examining them to test their texture, smoking a long, pale cigar and saying nothing, a tanned bald man in shorts and a pink and black Hawaiian shirt.

The manager announced his bid at the very end. It was for five thousand dollars, nearly twice as much as the other bids. The man's name was George Kanarsis and he was from Miami.

Following the rules of the auction, the manager asked if the bid was satisfactory. Grandfather would gladly have accepted any of the other bids, but something about George

Kanarsis — the way he rolled the long, pale cigar from one corner of his mouth to the other or the flashy way he was dressed or the way he eyed the towering stack of sponges as if he already owned them — made Grandfather balk.

The day was blisteringly hot, and Grandfather was sitting in the shade of the only tree in the courtyard. He got up and hobbled over to where Kanarsis and I were talking about the quality of the sponge.

"What will you do with the sponge," Grandfather asked Kanarsis, "should we sell them?"

Kanarsis was clearly surprised at the question. He took the cigar out of his mouth, tapped the ash from its end, put it back in his mouth, and rolled it around. Through the smoke he squinted at Grandfather.

"What difference does it make?" he said. "A sponge is a sponge. Whether a housewife in Chicago buys it for her kitchen or a horseman in Virginia buys it for his horses or someone washes a window with it somewhere in Indiana." George Kanarsis was annoyed. I looked for him to withdraw his bid.

"These are special sponges," I broke in. "We would like them to go to special markets and I am sure they will."

"I understand," Kanarsis said, relieved. "I'm president of the Carnation Cosmetic Company of Maine. We're introducing a new tropical face cream. As an added inducement, I plan to include a sponge with each purchase. Not a whole one, of course, but one the size of a lady's hand, nicely trimmed in a heart shape and scented, appropriate for the bathroom."

Grandfather said, "You have sponge enough?"

"A warehouse filled from floor to ceiling with sponges," Kanarsis said. "But I would like more of the wools. That is why I have made a special bid."

The manager came up. He was impatient. "Accept or not, Dimitrios," he said.

Grandfather didn't like the manager, who was new at the job, young, and not a Greek. He didn't like George Kanarsis, either. He was ready to refuse the five-thousand-dollar bid and accept the one for twenty-six hundred.

The deal hung in the balance. Grandfather glanced at the sponges. He hesitated, trying to make a decision. I made it for him before he could speak.

"We accept the Kanarsis bid," I said to the manager.

It startled Grandfather. He blinked. He started to shake his head. Then, seeing the set of my jaw, he changed his mind.

George Kanarsis smiled. He reached into the pocket of his pink and black shirt and took out a case made of alligator skin, clicked it open, and offered Grandfather one of his pale cigars.

Grandfather didn't smoke, but he took two of the cigars anyway, placing one in his mouth and the other in the crown of the straw hat he was wearing.

"Remember," Kanarsis said, "that I am interested in wool sponge. I'll buy all you bring in. I'd rather buy them outright, however, and not go through the bother of bidding."

"Bidding is good," Grandfather said.

"We'll talk about that later," Kanarsis said. "In the meantime, what can I do to help? You've got a small crew, I understand."

Grandfather rolled the cigar around in his mouth, copying Kanarsis.

"A couple more men?"

Grandfather shook his head.

"Another diver?"

"No men, no diver."

"When do you go again?" Kanarsis asked.

"Maybe a week. Sooner, maybe. When do I get the five thousand dollars?"

"The manager has the five thousand."

I took hold of Grandfather's arm and helped him across the courtyard toward the manager's office.

"I wonder about his check," he said, speaking in Greek. "Somehow I don't trust the man."

"We'll go to the bank," I said. "We'll cash his check before we turn over the sponges."

The manager had the payment ready for us. Lying on the counter were ten five-hundred-dollar bills, crisp and new, sitting in a stack.

We didn't go to the bank, as I wanted to do. Grandfather had no faith in banks. Instead, we took the money home and he dug a deep hole in the garage floor, wrapped the money in plastic, and buried it, with two old tires hiding the place.

# ❦ 13

We gave Steve Parsons and Tasso their shares, bought provisions for the boat, and sailed three days later. We left behind on the quay at least a dozen men who, attracted by our success, begged to be taken along.

We sailed toward the Middle Bank, but stopped a day short of where we had worked before. Grandfather felt certain that the boats from Key West had picked the place clean.

For a morning we cast the lead, searching for a reef that my father had worked once with good results. At noon, in a bright sun that made the bottom visible, we found it by sight and I went down at once in forty feet of water.

It was very clear on the bottom, with black sand underfoot and a line of low hillocks rolling out to the west. A mild current was moving in that direction.

In the light that filtered down from the sun, two-pronged

coral sparkled and cast off moving shadows. Fish were everywhere, more than I had ever seen. Groupers, their cavernous mouths open, swam past me warily. But a school of gold angelfish glided up, brushing against my lifeline, peering into all of the helmet's windows, curious about my bare hands that looked ghostly white.

There was no sponge in view except for a garden patch of honeycomb too young to harvest. I walked on, skirting a deep blue place that turned out to be a valley connecting two hills, and came to an immense stand of wool sponge. It stretched out to the west like a field of tassled corn.

We were in this field for three days, harvesting as much sponge as we had at the first location. By midmorning of the second day we had also collected nine sponge boats. They had followed us at a distance since the morning we left port. Off to the west, a shrimper was trawling at the edge of the Middle Bank.

All of the sponge boats were from Tarpon, manned by men we knew. After supper they got out their zithers and bouzoukia and played Greek tunes until midnight. Now and then someone started a song and everyone picked it up, including Grandfather.

The shrimper was anchored a mile or two away. Its lights shone across the water and once, when an airplane flew over, its searchlights swept the black sky. I kept thinking that the ship would hear our music and join us, but she never left her mooring.

A wind came up in the night and I didn't dive the next day. We cleaned sponge instead and hung them in the rigging to dry in the strong wind. The third day I went down in clear water as the sun rose.

It was close to noon and I had let a burst of air into the suit, making ready to go to the surface, when I saw a huge shadow directly above me. Objects underwater are magnified in size. At first I thought it was the bottom of our boat. Then the shadow moved, and at the same moment I saw both the boat and the shadow.

I let more air into the suit and left the bottom at once, yet cautiously, careful not to overtake the chain of bubbles from my helmet rising slowly above me. If I did, it would mean that I was ascending too fast and risked the deadly bends.

The shadow changed shape. For a moment it disappeared off to my left, ahead of the boat. Then it came back into view, at a lower level this time. Then it disappeared again and returned, swimming slowly.

The creature was circling the boat. There was no sign that it had seen me. The sun shone directly above and its reflected light made it impossible to tell v'hether this was a leopard shark or a shovelnose or one of the big white ones. All I could see were shifting shades of yellow and black, a dark gray shadow.

I was going up deliberately now. I had at least sixty more feet to go before I reached the boat.

The shadow made a third slow circle. This time it left a wave behind it and I felt the disturbed water swirl against my lifeline. There was no point in using the line to signal the men. There was nothing they could do. I was ascending as fast as I dared.

It was possible that the men had seen the shadow. Parsons carried a gun, but it would not be deadly at fathoms under the surface. The shots would do no more than rile the circling monster. I prayed that Parsons wouldn't use it.

The suit had grown terribly hot, and I was sweating from the heat and from fear. I recalled that in all the history of diving in the Gulf, not a single diver of thousands had ever been attacked by a shark. For some reason the thought did not lessen my fear.

I had a sponge knife strapped to my leg. I unfastened the strap and took a firm grip on the handle of the steel blade.

There was a lull. The water above me grew clear and calm except for the rising bubbles glittering in the sun. I let more air into the suit and began to move faster, yet for all my fear at a careful rate.

The lull lasted for less than a minute. I could see the bottom of the boat distinctly now, the oxblood red and the blue stripe marking the waterline. Then, as I felt a current pressing against my legs, I glanced down through the center window. Half the distance to the sea bottom, I saw the shape swimming slowly toward me, not in a straight line, more in an awkward spiral.

It was not a shark of any variety I had ever seen. In size it looked more like one of the big bottlenose dolphins but lacked their flashing blue and white markings.

The water around me was roiling now and in motion. I lost sight of the creature for an instant, then it appeared directly in front of me, not ten feet away. I was looking into the cold, black-flecked eyes of a mammoth loggerhead turtle.

My father had killed a loggerhead once and towed it into Tarpon and put it on display, but he was not in a diving suit when he killed it. He shot it with a high-powered rifle from the deck of a boat. This one was much bigger than the loggerhead he shot. It might weigh all of a thousand pounds.

It would take five minutes or more to get to the boat. There was little chance that I could reach it before the loggerhead attacked me. If he got tangled in my air hose, I would drown here in thirty feet of water.

With a jerk of my head I shut the air valve. The suit deflated and I was sinking toward the bottom. The loggerhead followed me, pulling slowly with its front flippers, pushing with the back ones.

The thought came to me that the turtle was only curious, curious about the boat and now about me. I remembered the octopus that had held out a tentacle and gently pressed my finger.

Then, as I met the monster's cold, unblinking stare, I remembered from my zoology class that turtles were reptiles, descendants of an ancient, venomous family.

My feet sank into milky white sand. Behind me, two branches of an elkhorn coral spread out against a ledge. I moved back against the coral and the rocky ledge. Protected from the back and on two sides, I knew it was a good place to make a stand. I didn't want to go farther out and take the chance of fouling my air hose.

The loggerhead had trailed me. It was so close now that I could see the small, neat patterns on the bulging skull, a skull twice the size of mine. The curved beak, which could snap an oar in two, opened every minute or so and then closed with a dull, clicking sound.

I had the knife in my hand. But there was not a single place on the carapace to sink it. The knife would break against armor that must have been two inches thick.

The monster was treading water, barely moving its flippers. I recalled that turtles breathe like human beings, not through gills like fish, but can stay underwater much longer than humans.

The diving suit was terribly hot. Sweat ran off me, and I could feel it collecting in my boots. I had been down now for nearly an hour. My shoulders felt as though I were holding up a heavy stone.

The loggerhead did not move. My knife was useless. Then I realized that the eyes staring at me were vulnerable.

I settled my feet firmly in the loose sand, the two branches of the elkhorn coral against my back, and raised the knife. I sighted along the steel blade. I would take one step forward and in the same moment thrust the knife deep into the monster's left eye, which was the one nearer.

Before I could make a move, the turtle came closer, so close that I felt the soft currents its flippers made against my bare hands. It was too close now for me to use the knife. The creature's eyes, deep brown rimmed with gold, stared at me. Through the thick window that separated us, I stared back.

Stale air backed up in my helmet. I began to feel terribly light-headed and I forgot how long I had been down. My limbs grew heavy and seemed to change their shape. Time disappeared in a dizzy spiral, taking me into a distant and forgotten past where I felt like an armored creature myself.

A frantic tug on the lifeline brought me to my senses and I put the knife back in its scabbard. Letting air out of the suit, I went up twenty feet and rested for ten minutes. Then I let more air out and rose to the diving platform and sat there with my feet trailing in the sea.

The big turtle had followed along in my wake. Now it was swimming back and forth, watching me with its gold-rimmed eyes. After a while it swam away.

## ❧ 14

The next day was too windy to dive. We spent the time cleaning the rest of our sponges and hanging them up to dry.

Something about the sandy bottom and the currents at this location made them hard to clean. From one of average size I shook out a dozen hairy crabs, a small starfish, and hundreds of tiny shrimp that had found shelter in the maze of chambers, canals, and tunnels that the sponge affords.

Late that afternoon, Spyros sent the launch with a note, asking us, Grandfather and me, to have dinner with him on the *Melina*. Grandfather held back as he had the first time, but the launch was waiting, nudging the side of our boat. So I got aboard and sat down. Only then did he decide to go.

Tasso and Steve Parsons were disappointed that they hadn't been invited. Parsons said, "Deckhands aren't good enough to go." Tasso said, "We only do the dirty work."

It was a sedate dinner, this time in the main cabin, unlike the wild celebration we'd had before. The table was set with gleaming silver and glass that sparkled like diamonds and a big bouquet of red, long-stemmed roses.

I had never seen so much food. Waiters brought in tray after tray and none of it came from the sea except a bowl of caviar in a bed of cracked ice. I had never eaten caviar before, but I didn't let on. I watched Spyros eat his first, spreading it on a cracker and adding a drop of lemon juice, before I ate mine. I didn't reveal that I was dazzled by all the splendor.

And I should have been hungry. In the morning on days I was diving I never had more than a cup of coffee. At noon I ate nothing and at night a cup of fish soup. Food is poison to a diver. It stays in your stomach and hurts more and more the deeper and longer you dive. I had been living on scant rations for days now, but I picked at the food the waiters brought.

Spyros took notice. "You don't like our cooking? What is it, Miss Alexandra? Just let me know and I'll see that it's changed when you come again."

He had said "when you come again." My cheeks flushed. Suddenly a series of festive meals stretched before me — flowers and twinkling glass and caviar — and, and Spyros next to me, sitting like an Athenian god.

"Oh, no, don't change anything," I said, surprised that suddenly I was no longer tongue-tied. "The food is wonderful. It's just that I dived today more than I should have and I don't feel very hungry."

"Tell us about the loggerhead that attacked you today," Grandfather said.

"It didn't attack me," I replied.

"Well, it chased you," Grandfather said. He was speaking in Greek because he was ashamed to speak his English in front of Spyros. "It was getting ready to attack the boat, then it spotted you and . . ."

"Followed me to the bottom," I said. "And then back to the boat."

"I caught glimpses of the thing," Grandfather said to Spyros. "It was as broad as this table and must have weighed a ton."

Spyros blinked in astonishment. "You're lucky, Alexandra, you might have been hurt. On my last trip to Panama, I heard about a diver attacked by a hawksbill. He fought the turtle for over an hour and finally killed it by stabbing it in the eye."

"That's the only way you can kill these monsters," Grandfather said. "Alexandra had a knife, but she let the thing get away."

"Why?" Spyros asked. "It will hang around for days, as long as you're here. They do that."

"Because it was only following me around. It never tangled the air hose. It was just curious, I guess. It never tried to harm me."

"The loggerhead may be around when you dive again," Spyros said. "They have sharp and powerful beaks. He may snap a hand off — both your hands — and tear up your air hose. I have seen them bite a clamshell in two — a shell as thick as the top of this table — as if it were a stick of peppermint. How do you know that it won't be down there waiting for you?"

"I don't."

At these words, Spyros shook his head. After that he seemed to lose interest in the turtle, and though Grandfather urged me to go on with the story, I said nothing more.

Three times while we were finishing dinner Spyros was called to the bridge. The third time he was gone for a while and when he came back he excused himself, kissed me on the forehead, and sent us back to the boat with a large piece from the six-layered cake wrapped up carefully in tinfoil for Steve Parsons and Tasso. It seemed an odd thing for him to do.

I was too excited to sleep. From my sleeping bag spread out on the cabin top, where I always slept, I watched the riding lights of the *Melina*. I went over every minute, every second, of the evening and when I fell asleep near dawn, I dreamed of Spyros Stavaronas. He was the god Poseidon and he was on a ship. The ship was sailing along the shore of Kalymnos. And there I was on a promontory by the blue sea, basking on a sunny rock — a mermaid with streaming hair, with white, gleaming flesh instead of fishy scales.

Then the god waved to me and I waved back. But the ship went sailing on beyond the promontory and slowly out of view. That was the dream that came to me as I slept. I woke disturbed, to find that the *Melina* had disappeared in the night.

# ❧ 15

I picked wool sponge for two more days and we sailed home with a bigger harvest than before. George Kanarsis was at the auction — dressed in his pink and black Hawaiian shirt and smoking one of his long, pale cigars. This time he made a bid of six thousand dollars, which we accepted.

We paid the commission on the sale to the Sponge Exchange and gave Steve Parsons and Tasso their shares. It was a muggy day and to celebrate, Grandfather and I went down to the ice cream parlor across the street from the Lighthouse Café and ordered Idiot's Delights, which have three scoops of vanilla and one scoop of coconut, sprinkled with walnuts, pecans, and filberts at twenty cents extra if you want them, topped with persimmon syrup and whipped cream.

We were nearly through when a brand-new car done up in flame-colored metallic paint parked in front of the café. It was a towaway zone, but the car parked nevertheless and Steve Parsons and Tasso got out.

Tasso was carrying a radio the size of a valise, tuned to a rock station in Tampa. It sounded loud even from across the street.

Steve Parsons had on a new pair of yellow cowboy boots and a ten-gallon hat that had a chicken-feather hatband decorated with what looked to be the rattles of a big rattlesnake. He was wearing a Hawaiian shirt something like the pink and black one Kanarsis wore and he was smoking one of Kanarsis' long, pale cigars.

"How much do we pay those two?" Grandfather asked. He was getting forgetful. He had given the men their shares less than an hour before.

"You took out expenses for the boat and money for food," I said. "Their shares came to twelve hundred dollars. On the first trip they made nine hundred. How they divided the money, I don't know."

"They divided too much. Now they'll be asking for more. But they won't get more. They'll sit around in the Lighthouse Café and drink until their money's gone."

Grandfather was wrong. When we finished our Idiot's Delights, I ran across the street and told Steve Parsons that we were going out the following day at sunrise.

I waited for him to ask for a greater share of the profits. He never mentioned money.

"Sunrise," Tasso said, "is awful soon."

"We'll be there," Steve Parsons said, "bright-eyed and bushy-tailed."

I didn't expect this answer and I didn't expect to see them at the wharf. But they were there, if not bright-eyed, at least on their feet and anxious to go.

Parsons had bought a rifle in the meantime, and he had it wrapped up in a fancy sheepskin case. I didn't know what he was carrying until Grandfather asked him about it.

"A thirty-ought-six," Parsons said. "Shoots as fast as you can squeeze your fist."

"Fast," Tasso said, making a buzzing sound with a finger in his mouth.

"What you do with the rifle?" Grandfather asked.

"Kill the loggerhead if it bothers us again," Parsons said. "Or sharks. We're lucky so far with the sharks."

The two men had worked hard since the day we brought the first boatload of wool sponge to the auction and sold it for a record price. On the second trip they worked just as hard. On this third trip they were on deck fifteen hours a day, sorting sponges, cleaning them more thoroughly than they had before, stringing them in graded wreaths, being sure that the wreaths were properly strung up to dry. They put me into my diving suit with great care. And when I was on the bottom I had the feeling, which I had never had before, that they were watching the air hose, guarding the lifeline as if they themselves were ten fathoms deep in a dangerous sea.

Parsons, when he wasn't working or sleeping, had the rifle out, firing at sea gulls and imaginary sharks, talking about his new supercharged car that would do a hundred miles an hour in fourth gear. Tasso had his radio blaring most of the time, trying out different stations, some as far away as Cuba.

The two men got along well except for once, during supper the second day out, when they fell into an argument about the new car.

"I want a car," Tasso said.

"You've got a car already. You drive around with me all the time," Parsons said. "After you learn to drive yourself and get a license, you can drive it anytime you want to."

"I want my own car," Tasso said. In the light from the oil drum I saw his hands tighten. The cat's eyes on his knuckles seemed to glitter. "And I won't get a car until I have more shares than I get now."

"We'll see," Parsons said. "If there's another bid like the last two, I'll give you a bonus. Remember, man, three months ago you'd never been near the sea, let alone a sponge."

Tasso spat over the rail. "Don't forget the bonus."

"I'll try," Parsons said, putting the rifle to his shoulder, aiming into the dark through the telescopic sight, and firing a round of shots.

"Spongin's no good now," Tasso said.

"It'll get better," Parsons said.

It didn't. The first two days were good, but the wools ran out the third morning and all I sent up from the reef were browns and flowerpots. There were a lot of these. In the next two days we spent on the reef we filled the boat. There were so many flowerpots and browns that we improvised a raft, stacked it with the sponge, and tied it to the stern.

Shortly after dawn, while we were getting ready to leave, I saw the loggerhead turtle swimming behind the raft. I had caught a glimpse of it the morning before, feeding in a clump of elkhorn sponge. Then later it had followed me up, and when I stopped and rested at six fathoms it came and swam around me, turning its head from side to side, peering in the tiny windows. In the morning sun the patterns on its back glittered and its eyes looked more golden than they had in the murky depths.

It circled the boat and swam back to where I was working on the raft. Apparently Steve Parsons had been watching the creature, too, for he suddenly appeared on the stern and, before I could raise my voice, aimed his rifle, pressed the trigger, and sent a shower of bullets into the turtle.

It turned over on one side, then onto its back. And then it slid slowly from sight, leaving a bright patch of blood.

Steve Parsons said something to Tasso and they both laughed. Grandfather was down in the cabin, asleep. I waited for a while, busying myself with the raft, until Parsons laid the rifle out to clean it and went aft for something. Then I walked back to where it lay on top of the cabin, picked it up, and in front of Tasso's startled eyes threw the thirty-ought-six into the water. It sank much faster than the big turtle.

The voyage back to Tarpon was silent. The two men stayed down in the cabin and didn't come up until we reached Anclote Key.

We didn't have any hope for our cargo. Nine tenths of it was sponge of inferior quality. We arranged the wreaths in the courtyard to make the best show possible, the wool sponges in front and the rest out of sight, more or less.

Kanarsis was on hand. The morning was again blisteringly

hot, and he wore a floppy straw hat so big that it hid his face and all you could see was the long, pale cigar sticking out. He walked around the pile of sponges, picked out one or two, tossed them back, and walked away, slowly puffing his cigar.

"If we're lucky, very lucky," Grandfather said, "we'll come out with a thousand dollars."

Twelve bids were handed in. Kanarsis didn't bid at first, and we thought for a while that he wasn't going to bid at all. He walked around our stack again and at last wrote out a slip, signed it, and handed it in.

The manager, as he had before, read the other bids first. They were all for less than a thousand dollars. George Kanarsis' bid was for three thousand three hundred.

I thought Grandfather would be elated to receive three or four times the amount he expected. But all he did when the manager gave him his money, minus the commission, was to say thank you. Kanarsis offered him a cigar, which he refused.

Tasso and Steve Parsons were waiting in the courtyard. We paid them and they went off, speeding down Dodecanese Street. Nothing was said about the rifle.

I watched them drive away, then I said, "I'd like a car."

"We have a car," Grandfather said.

"A new one, not a clunker."

"New cars cost money."

"All of the sponge was picked by me," I reminded him. "So my share should be more than Parsons'."

"He didn't have enough money to pay cash. He must have bought the car on credit."

"What credit?" I asked. "He's from another state. He hasn't been in Tarpon Springs for more than five months. Who would give him credit for an expensive car?"

"Somebody who's not very smart," Grandfather said.

The day was hot, so we went down to the ice cream parlor. Parsons and Tasso came back along Dodecanese Street to show off the car, going about ten miles an hour with the radio blaring. We were sitting by the window and they waved to us.

# ❀ 16

I paid our check with my last three dollars — Grandfather
had not yet paid me for diving — and we walked down to
the river.

A crowd of tourists stood on the wharf gazing at *Cybele*.
A guide was telling them over a loudspeaker about the boat
and the Greek girl who had braved dire dangers — storms,
sharks, octopus, an encounter with a giant turtle half the size
of the boat — a girl who with her crippled grandfather had
wrested a fortune from the perilous sea.

Catching sight of us, the guide waved. I grasped Grandfather's arm and we disappeared up Dodecanese Street and
did not return to the boat until the crowd had left.

The guide was still there, standing on the wharf. He had
a bullhorn in his hand and was shouting the same words I
had heard before. I recognized him as Pete Damaskinos, the

son of a diver, a dark-visaged, unsmiling young man who had tried diving and given it up after an attack of the bends. People called him "the Thinker" because of his habit of stopping whatever he was doing to stare blankly into space.

He stopped shouting and tipped his cap to me. "I hope you don't mind," he said. "It's a job. I've made ten dollars while you were away at the auction, just talking. You could leave the boat here during the time you're not out sponging. And I could show it, take people aboard. I can make fifty dollars a day. I'll divide it with you. We could make a lot more if you sat down there at the tiller in your diving suit. You could hold the helmet in your lap and answer people's questions, like, "How do you feel down in the water with sharks swimming around you?"

I tried to visualize myself sitting at the tiller in my diving suit, holding the heavy helmet in my lap, anwering questions.

Damaskinos paused as he saw the painful look on my face, but he went on nonetheless. "Sponging's bad. You never know when a storm's going to take you. You may not work for weeks at a time. Or you might have trouble down there and end up dead or crippled for life, like me. Nine out of ten who dive in the Gulf end up that way. But with this you'd just sit and look pretty and answer questions. Then after a while we might spread out. We could sell trips at three dollars a ticket, take twenty-five passengers out to the bayou. We'd plant sponge out there in ten feet of water, and you could go down and bring up a sackful and I'd sell them for five dollars apiece. Make six trips a day."

Grandfather groaned.

"There's a thing like that already," I said. My mother sells tickets for the trips. She has a booth on Dodecanese."

"I know, and they're making a fortune," he said. "But you're a celebrity. Your picture has been in the papers. And you're a woman. They have a man, an old man. Tourists would flock here by the thousands to see you."

As he paused, waiting for an answer, I heard the squealing of brakes. The sound came from across the river, not a hundred yards away, and I saw Steve Parsons in his flashy Hawaiian shirt step out of the car and disappear into the office of the Stavaronas Shrimp Company.

Tired of waiting for me to say something, Damaskinos was shouting over the loudspeaker again. Three women in billed caps were coming toward me, shading their eyes against the sunlight that bounced off the river. All of them were carrying cameras.

I grasped Grandfather's arm and got him on the boat, started the motor, untied the mooring lines, and headed out into the river just as the three women arrived on the wharf. They waved and I waved back.

Grandfather had not heard the squealing brakes nor noticed Steve Parsons go into the office of the Stavaronas Shrimp Company. As we approached the plant and the big white shrimper, *Sweet Melina,* moored at the dock, I told him what I had seen.

"Do you suppose that Parsons is in there asking Spyros for a job?" I said.

"Not so long as Kanarsis buys sponge from us at fancy prices and Parsons's getting his share of the money."

"But that may end soon. Kanarsis is a mystery to me."

"To me also."

"He can change his mind. His face cream can flop."

We passed the shrimp company. The red car was there on the wharf. Tasso was playing his radio, walking along the wharf, kicking a can he had found along the way. Steve Parsons was still in the office.

Mother was cooking supper when we got home. The first thing she said was that Pete Damaskinos had come to see her during the afternoon while she was selling tickets for the river trip and sponge diving.

"I think he has a good idea," she said. "We have more business than we can handle. I sold one hundred and sixty-five tickets today at two dollars and a half a ticket. I could have sold fifty more. Mr. Angelakis is raising the price to three dollars beginning next Saturday and he's thinking about putting on another boat." She had onions in a pan and they were burning. "Damaskinos has a good idea."

"A terrible idea," Grandfather said.

"Wonderful." Daphne, who was watching TV, tossed the word over her shoulder.

Mother threw out the burned onions, sliced another batch, and put them in the skillet. "It's better," she said, "than death or something worse than death that comes to all who sail the unfriendly waters of the Gulf."

"What do you say to this?" Grandfather growled at me. "You have said nothing so far. Say that you have conquered the dark waters and laughed at death. Tell this to your mother, Athena. Tell her that you are a true daughter of Kalymnos."

"My mother turned to look at me.

"Speak up," Grandfather commanded me. "Are you or are you not a child of Kalymnos?"

"I am," I said quietly.

My mother turned away. As she stood at the stove, she said nothing more.

A shrimper went by, going toward Anclote Key and the Gulf. My heart leaped at the sound. I ran to the window and looked out. The ship had gone.

Daphne said, not bothering to look around, "It's not Spyros. We have a date tonight."

## 🌿 17

Without saying a word to us, Steve Parsons and Tasso suddenly disappeared the next day. We worried that they had decided to work for the Stavaronas Shrimp Company. But three days later, while I was carrying provisions aboard the boat, just as we had decided to go without them, they showed up, eager to sail. It seemed they had been shopping in Tampa. Parsons was wearing a new waterproof wristwatch and Tasso had a pair of expensive binoculars dangling from his neck.

We had cleaned out the wool sponge on the reef where I had dived before. Beyond this place, the reef ended in a rocky cliff, and at the bottom was a small gray valley of elkhorn coral mingled with stands of wool sponge, but they were deeper than I wanted to go. The pressure there would be frightening. A few of our divers dared these depths — my father had been one — but they were very dangerous.

It took us a day and a half to reach the grounds. Late in the afternoon I made my first dive and came back to the surface to tell Grandfather what I had seen.

"The water is clear and I could see a valley of wool sponge, more than we've taken so far," I said. "I might try it down there for ten minutes or so."

Grandfather shook his head. "Since Kanarsis seems to be satisfied with any variety, let's not take chances. Let's go back to the old reef and fill up with flowerpots and wires — perhaps a few wools."

The place was six hours' sailing due south from where we were. We got there at dawn of the following day, and as the sun came up in an overcast sky, I made my first dive in six fathoms of brilliantly clear water. Sponge grew thick along a level ridge. The footing of pink gravel was good, and the current flowing in from the south was so gentle that I could walk rapidly through the field.

In two days the boat was loaded with sponge. When I wasn't in the water, Steve Parsons and Tasso sweated, cleaning the catch. Parsons would pause now and again to dunk his waterproof watch in the sea and then examine it to find out if it was really waterproof. Tasso cleaned sponges with the binoculars hanging around his neck. We all worked late into the night, cleaning sponge by lanterns strung from the rigging.

Steve Parsons said, "No telling when the man will stop buying. Maybe this trip, maybe the next."

"Who knows?" Tasso said. It seemed to sum up the situation for them as well as for Grandfather and me. We were working against time and chance — and the whim of George Kanarsis.

By late afternoon of the fifth day, thin white clouds streamed in from the west and covered the sky. Night came on, black and starless. Grandfather thought we should sail for home, but we overruled him.

I asked Tasso to turn on his radio and he brought in a weather report from Tampa. There was a storm two hundred miles west of us, traveling in our direction at five miles an hour.

"We can leave tomorrow noon, outrun it to Anclote Key," I said.

"What if the storm picks up?" Grandfather said.

"It's just a storm, not a hurricane," Parsons said.

"You a weatherman?"

"I've seen a lot of weather," Parsons replied.

"We can outrun it," I said. "I'll go down early, at sunrise. We'll make five more wreaths and by noon we'll be headed home."

At the tiller, Grandfather Stefanos watched the skies and never for a moment dreamed why I was so bent on diving again. It was a risky decision. The storm might overtake us and we could lose our cargo.

Besides, I was very tired. The thought of sliding into the heavy suit, which by now smelled to heaven, was abhorrent. Even more abhorrent was the thought of dragging on the ponderous boots with the lead soles and brass-tipped toes, holding my breath as the helmet clamped shut over my head and the copper studs were wrenched tight, and I peered out of the four little windows like a prisoner in a barred cell while the air hose hissed in my ears like an angry snake.

Early that morning I had seen the big white shrimper cruising far down on the horizon. Then again in the afternoon it had appeared to the south of us, much closer this time. I was certain that by nightfall the ship would anchor nearby, as it had in the past, and that Spyros would send the launch for us.

I even dreamed that he would send it only for me, and quietly I would defy Grandfather and depart for the ship alone. I saw him standing at the rail, gazing down at me, handsome in his white uniform, waiting as I stepped onto the deck, the god Poseidon himself — anxious to kiss me, not upon the brow as he had before but upon my eager lips.

I gave up my dream when the launch came with an invitation addressed to Stefanos Dimitrios and Miss Alexandra Dimitrios in the exact words Spyros had used the time before.

He was not at the rail. One of the two young men who ran the launch led us to a cabin between the dining room and the bridge, excused himself, and came back with word that the captain was on the phone and would join us as soon as he had finished his call.

"We ran into a school of gray snapper this afternoon," the boatman said. "Brought up six ton by accident. Captain Stavaronas is trying to find a market. We're full up with shrimp and can't refrigerate six tons of fish. We've got to get them off our hands by tomorrow. So far, no luck."

He excused himself and disappeared. In a moment I heard the launch start up. The motor idled for a time and then stopped, and I heard the young man come back on deck.

Thinking that his actions might have something to do with the weather, I went outside. Nothing had changed. The wind was still blowing in gusts from the west. The sky was starless. On the way back to the cabin, I met the young man and asked him if he had a late report on the weather. He shook his head and without a word went on along the passageway. I heard the launch start up again.

When I got back to the cabin, Spyros was talking to Grandfather about the weather. Minutes passed before he realized that I was in the room. Then he stopped talking, clicked his heels, and made a stiff bow, as if I were the queen of England and not a girl in love.

For a brief moment I was sorry I had come.

# ☙ 18

Dinner was not nearly so lavish as the one before, and I could see that Spyros was worried about the storm. He kept jumping up to go outside to look at the sky. Every five minutes someone would come down from the bridge with a weather report. Finally, he went to the bridge himself. When he came back, he didn't sit down but stood in the doorway.

"They've given her a name," he said. "She's called Dolores, which means officially she's a hurricane. A small one, but still a hurricane. Sometimes they blow themselves out after twenty-four hours, sometimes they don't. I've decided to leave for Anclote. It might be wise for you to do the same, Stefanos Dimitrios."

Stumbling over his chair, Grandfather got to his feet. "We will go also." In his eagerness to leave he forgot and spoke in his halting English, which embarrassed him. He paused, then said in Greek, "I wished to leave this afternoon when the storm was reported, but Alexandra talked me into staying on."

"Why?"

"She wants to dive again in the morning."

"Dive?" Spyros said. He put an arm around my shoulders. "Alexandra has become a real fish." He paused and gave me an admiring look. "An angelfish. The one with the big eyes that change colors in the sunlight and the mouth that has a gay lift to it—a sort of angelic smile. Is she always an angel?"

"Sometimes," Grandfather said.

Spyros pressed my shoulder as he took his arm away. I quit breathing. The ship was rocking, or was it my heart? Then he asked how fast *Cybele* could go, and I managed to tell him that she could make seven knots without sails.

"In these winds with the sails she should make another knot," he said. "I'll have the launch take you back. Use the sails and follow my wake."

"That is nice of you," I said stiffly.

"We'll leave in half an hour. At nine-thirty exactly."

"We'll be ready," Grandfather said. He limped to the door and turned to face Spyros. "Is it possible for Alexandra to call her mother? Her mother is a great worrier about storms. It would ease her mind to know that we are on our way home."

Spyros said immediately, "The channels are cluttered up now. I doubt that we can get through. I'll try a little later when we're on our way. Around ten would be a good time. I'll call then and tell her that you'll be home by midnight tomorrow."

"You know our number," I said. "You have called it before."

Spyros nodded.

The radio operator also knew the number. He had overheard our conversation, and as we started to leave the cabin, he called down from the bridge that he had been able to get through and that Mrs. Dimitrios was on the line.

I hurried up the ladder. The operator got up from his console and handed me the receiver. At first there was a lot of noise on the line — static, strange mutterings — then the line cleared and I heard my mother's voice.

"Where are you, Alexandra?"

The operator, who was standing nearby, overheard us and gave me the approximate longitude and latitude, which I repeated over the phone.

"I make nothing of that," she said, excited at the call. "Where are you?"

The operator told me the distance and the general direction. "One hundred and twenty-six miles west of Anclote Key," I said. "We'll be home by midnight tomorrow."

"You know about the storm?"

"We do and we're leaving now."

"I forgot to ask where you're calling from."

"From Spyros' ship."

In the next breath, Daphne was on the phone. Her voice came in clear and sharp. She didn't bother to say hello.

"Let me speak to Spyros," she said.

I got up to call him, but he was standing right behind me.

He took the phone, pressed the receiver hard against his ear, and turned from me and lowered his voice so I couldn't hear the conversation. I stepped away, as far as the steering wheel, yet I heard most of the words, even Daphne's.

She said, "Have you forgotten that we have a date tonight? We're supposed to have dinner and go to that tacky charity dance. It was your idea."

"I tried to call you earlier today, this afternoon," Spyros said. "I couldn't get through on account of the weather. We've been tied up here for two days by an unexpected haul of snapper. Tons of fish that are too valuable to destroy."

There was a short silence. I was facing the ship's bow. A trail of phosphorescence stretched away on the dark sea, and I saw that it had been made by *Sweet Melina*'s launch. The boat was now below, waiting at the landing steps. I didn't move.

Daphne's voice was gentle for a time after that. "I am glad," she said, "you have been able to entertain Alexandra and Grandfather."

Spyros said something in reply that I couldn't catch.

Daphne's words still came through slowly and soft. They always did when she was preparing to be mad.

"These dinners have become quite a habit," she said.

"It's fun to have Alexandra and your great old grandfather aboard."

"Apparently."

There was another silence, longer this time.

"Is it possible," Daphne said, stretching each word out, "that you're making a play for my baby sister?"

Spyros ran his fingers through his hair. He laughed. "Are you mad? Are you insane?"

"No, but you seem to be."

"Spyros Stavaronas making a play for a child? Come on, Daphne, be reasonable!"

Had he forgotten that I was there on the bridge? He must have or else he thought that when I handed him the phone I had left. For when he turned and saw me running from the bridge and down the ladder, he called my name, called it twice, but I didn't answer.

# ❧ 19

Steve Parsons and Tasso were waiting for us when we got back to the boat. They had stowed all the loose gear, cinched down the sponges, and had the buntlines ready to hoist the sails.

"Good," said Grandfather. "Very good!"

I was curious. "How did you know that we're leaving?" I asked them.

"The launchman told us the shrimper was leaving," Tasso said. "So I figured we would leave, too."

Steve Parsons said nothing.

We left at the appointed hour, our sails bellying to a stiff wind and the motor turning over at full throttle. We followed in the wake of the shrimper, heading for Anclote Key and the river.

The night was hot, and part of a moon shone through gauzy clouds. Grandfather stretched himself out on deck, where it was cooler than in the cabin. Steve Parsons and Tasso got up on the cabin roof, ready to trim sail if it became necessary. I sat at the stern, feet braced, and gripped the tiller in both hands.

I steered in silence, my eyes on the running lights ahead, on the trim of our sails, aware of the waves that surged up out of the darkness, lifted the boat, and passed on hissing under the keel. Not once did I think of Spyros Stavaronas, or if I did the thought passed as swiftly as the monstrous waves. But my heart was heavy, as if someone had stomped on it. And when Grandfather shouted, asking why I was so silent, I pretended I hadn't heard him.

We did not catch the full fury of the storm. It veered to the south like the one months before. Still, we were on its edges and suffered damage.

Rain began to fall near midnight in wind-driven gusts. Each of the sponges soaked up its share of water, rendering the boat topheavy. We were forced to take in sail and slow the engine to less than half speed.

Soon after midnight the shrimper circled back and pulled alongside. Its searchlight played across our deck from bow to stern — three times slowly.

Spyros shouted down to us, "You're listing to port. Are you in trouble?"

I cupped my hands and shouted back, "We're all right. Unless the wind builds up again."

He was standing at the rail, hidden in a yellow slicker and hood. I couldn't see his face. I didn't need to. It was graven on my heart. It would be there forever.

"The Tarpon radio reports less wind," he shouted down, "but I'll keep an eye on you."

I didn't answer. The ship went on and we followed her.

Through the night the wind blew in lessening gusts. The rain ceased. The sun rose in a cloudless sky, revealing the damage we had received in the night. Many of the wreaths had been broken and sponges littered the deck. Some had been blown away.

Soon after dawn, confident that we were safe though we still had a list to port, the shrimper sounded her air horn and disappeared toward Anclote Key.

With a fair wind and calmer seas, Grandfather took the tiller and I turned in to help Steve Parsons and Tasso repair the damage. I stamped the water out of the sponges one by one and passed them on for the men to restring and hang out to dry. I was determined to finish the task before I collapsed.

As I stamped water from the last of the sponges, I saw what looked to be a cigar wrapped in plastic film lying on the deck. I took it to be one that Steve Parsons had dropped by mistake.

I picked it up and was about to lay it aside to give to him when the plastic wrapping cracked and I saw that instead of tobacco it contained a white powder like sugar. Instantly, I thought of a movie I had seen at school about the dangers of cocaine. The powder in the movie and the powder I held in my hand looked exactly alike.

Yet I could have been mistaken. The sun was blinding.

The sea was taking up the hot light and casting it over the deck in distorted shapes and shadows. Then I remembered another thing from the movie. Cocaine was bitter. I broke open the package and put a speck of the powder on my tongue. It had a bitter taste.

Then, among a tangle of sponges wedged between a mooring cleat and the rail, I made out one twice the size of the others. From one of its large canals protruded the tip of a cigar-shaped tube like the one I held.

Parsons was working on the top of the cabin. Tasso was standing behind him at the rail. They were stringing the sponges that I had passed along. Neither of them was watching me. I pushed the tube back into the sponge until it was completely hidden. Then I put the other tube in my blouse and cleaned up the deck.

Tasso and Steve Parsons finished their job and stretched out on the top of the cabin. As soon as they fell asleep I examined a string of sponges, a dozen of them that they had carefully wrapped around the mast. All of them were big, and in the large canal of each one was a tube of pure cocaine, wrapped tightly and sealed by heat.

I no longer felt like sleeping. I made myself a pot of coffee and sat down with my back against the bowsprit and drank it out of the pot. I didn't stop to think about how the cocaine got on the boat nor about who had put it there. My only thought was about the danger if the drug was ever discovered. My only feeling was fear. Stark fear.

A Coast Guard plane flew over, and I took off the scarf that bound my hair and waved it as I always did.

I said nothing to Grandfather. If I told him, he would report it, and I wasn't sure that it should be reported. I needed time to think.

# ❧ 20

We sighted Anclote Key at dusk. But the wind died on us as we entered the river, and the overworked engine began to limp along on only one of its two cylinders. It was close to midnight before we saw my mother's signal fire and her standing on the wharf, a tall, black figure, to take the mooring lines that I tossed ashore.

The two men decided to stay on board for the night. Not to my surprise, for by now I was fairly certain that they had hidden the packets of deadly cocaine, hidden them away in the deep canals of the sponges. At least they knew about the operation.

It was a sweltering night, and Mother had prepared a cold supper, including the little Spanish sardines that Grandfather liked so much, the ones that swim side by side in yellow oil, their tiny gold eyes the size of pinpoints staring out at you.

I made a show of eating, but the food lingered in my

throat. My mother noticed it before the meal had barely begun.

"You're pale," she said. "And little wonder." She paused to cast an accusing glance at Grandfather Stefanos. "What with all the strain of diving and then on top of that the hurricane, it's a wonder you're still alive."

Grandfather said, "She is young, she is strong. She dives in the deep and comes back with smiles."

"But she does not eat her good food," Mother said. "And she is pale. You will not take her out again for a long time. We have enough money to last us through the winter — if someone hasn't stolen it from the hole you dug. Alexandra, my daughter, is going back to school. It begins next week. And next week she will be there. Unless, unless she comes down with one of the horrible things that lurk in the sea."

There are many horrible things you can come down with, I said to myself, in the sea and on the sea.

Suddenly a light shone through the window, a car door opened and closed. Then Daphne came rushing in, beautiful in a pink summer dress, smiling a small, mysterious smile. It was all of two minutes before she settled down and we learned why she looked so gay.

Daphne lit a cigarette and let the smoke curl out of her mouth and up her nose. I waited, wondering, for the smoke to come out, but it never did.

"We're engaged," she said at last. "Just an hour ago, and we're to be married next month on the tenth of October, my birthday. Isn't it wonderful?" She glanced at me.

"Wonderful," I said. I tried to smile to make her think that

I really meant it. The smile faded on my lips. Again I said, "Wonderful," then thought to add, "I am terribly happy for you, Daphne."

"You and Spyros Stavaronas," Grandfather said, "you will be happy people together."

On the night he first met Spyros, Grandfather had lost some of his hatred for the Stavaronas family. He lost more of it each time he went to the ship and sat down with Spyros to eat and drink. I think that at that moment, though he would never have said so, he really admired him.

I kissed Daphne goodnight and went to bed and slept soundly. But when I woke in the middle of the night I didn't know where I was. At first I was deep down in a troubled sea, stumbling among jagged coral and sponge that looked like severed heads. A current dragged relentlessly at my legs. Then I was at the tiller, staring into a vast darkness broken only by the distant lights of a great white ship.

In my mouth through it all was the ashen taste of disbelief and pain.

# 🎋 21

Daphne and my mother had left for work by the time I got myself out of bed. I still wasn't hungry, but I made a big breakfast for Grandfather and sat down with him while he ate it. It was another sweltering day, so we sat on the porch. The little air that stirred smelled of mangroves and river mud.

I could see our boat from where I sat, with Steve Parsons and Tasso asleep, stretched out on the cabin top. After a while Parsons roused himself, made a fire, and put something in a pan. While he was waiting for it to cook, he walked to his car, which was parked at the foot of the pier, and cleaned it off with a bucket of water and one of our sponges.

"That car cost money," Grandfather said.

"Twelve thousand dollars," I said. "At least that's what Tasso told me."

"And the watch that likes the water, what is the cost for that one? A hundred dollars?"

"More. Much more."

"Two hundred dollars, maybe?"

"Eleven hundred dollars."

"You heard this?"

"From Tasso."

"The rifle that has a telescope?"

I shrugged. "Perhaps six hundred."

Instead of swearing, Grandfather shouted, "Saint Nicolas in a rowboat!" and fell silent while he finished his omelet, into which I had stirred five eggs and two cloves of garlic.

Tasso was awake now, playing cowboy music on his radio. Steve Parsons was sitting with his pistol in his lap. Whenever a gull flew over he would lift the gun and take aim. They were waiting for us to finish breakfast and walk down to the boat and sail her up the river to the Sponge Exchange for the auction, which began in the morning at eleven o'clock.

The red car that glittered in the hot sun now that Parsons had cleaned it up was the first thing that had made me suspicious. No, not really suspicious, just curious. How could Steve Parsons scrape up enough money, I had wondered, to buy such an expensive car? A down payment would require more than the money Grandfather had paid him. Besides, Parsons was a drifter who would have had little or no credit at a bank. The rifle and the waterproof watch had only increased my curiosity.

"*Cybele*," Grandfather said. "She lists with the sponges. Trash, most of it."

"It makes no difference to Kanarsis," I said. "Half of what he bought last time was trash."

"Kanarsis. I think about Kanarsis. That man is crazy, maybe. Maybe he is crazy about you." Grandfather shook his head and gave up on his English. "Tell me," he said, "when you and Kanarsis were talking. That was the first time, before he made a bid. What did you talk about?"

"I don't remember exactly."

"He wasn't telling you how handsome you were and so forth?"

"So forth?"

"You know what I mean."

It was difficult for him to say the words — the four- and five- and six-letter words that every junior high and high school girl understood and many of them used. My parents were that way, too, my father, especially. They were afraid they might come out with something I had never heard or thought about before.

"When you were talking to Kanarsis, did you think he was up to no good?"

"Never. We talked about wool sponges, how beautiful they were, about his wonderful perfume and why he had named it Serpent's Secret."

Grandfather grasped his cane. He got slowly to his feet and took a few little steps to steady himself. "Now we bring the trash to market."

I couldn't say or even hint that it wasn't trash we were taking to market. There must have been dozens of packets of cocaine hidden away in the wreaths that festooned the rails. Each packet was worth, judging from the movie I had seen, thousands of dollars. If I told Grandfather that the boat was loaded with cocaine, he wouldn't hesitate to sail her straight up the river to the Coast Guard pier and hobble straight into the office and turn her over to Petty Officer Rogers.

There were several good reasons I didn't want this to happen. Grandfather, as he always did, would look at only one side of the problem. Unlike me, he believed that laws were made to be enforced — no matter what the consequences, whether it hurt innocent people or not. He was a long-bearded Moses when it came to the law.

I didn't care about Parsons and Tasso, whether they fled the country or spent a year or two in prison. But I did care about Grandfather. He had brought himself back to life by returning to the days of his youth. He took great pride in his being able to remember where the best sponges could be found. In his gathering boatload after boatload and selling them at auction for unheard-of prices. To inform him that the sponges were bought, not for their worth, but for the costly cocaine, would injure him deeply.

Surely the drugs came from the *Melina,* during the times we had spent on the ship. There were twelve or more men in the ship's crew. Any or all of them might be involved in the smuggling. But could the smuggling go on without Spyros ever knowing about it? Did the cocaine belong to him? Had he used our boat — used me also — to run it ashore and sell it to Kanarsis? My heart stopped at the thought.

And Daphne. If I reported the drugs to the Coast Guard and Spyros was arrested, what would become of her marriage?

I didn't like Daphne. If she hadn't been my sister, I would never have bothered to speak to her. But she *was* my sister. She was a part of the family. She was a part of me, the same as my right hand.

I didn't know which way to turn. I was scared and terribly confused. Besides everything else, the boat might be seized. We might be arrested for trafficking in drugs, even convicted and sent to prison.

The men were waiting for us. The engine was running, Tasso had untied the lines, and Parsons gave the throttle a push. They were anxious to reach the unloading wharf, to move the sponges safely ashore and into the auction courtyard.

# ✿ 22

At noon, after we had unloaded our cargo, I left Grandfather at the ice cream parlor. He liked to chat with the
pretty waitresses as much as he liked the ice cream. Then I
took the boat across the river and moored her at the Stavaronas Shrimp Company dock, just to the stern of the *Melina*.

I went ashore and asked one of the crew if Captain Stavaronas was on board. When he nodded, I found a patch of
shade and tried to catch my breath. I was burning up from
the awful heat.

I was standing in the shade, about to run a comb through
my hair, when I heard my name spoken. Looking up, I saw
Spyros leaning over the rail, his dark gaze fixed upon me.

"What are you doing out in all this heat?" he called down.

I started to answer.

"You should be in swimming."

"I want to talk to you," I said.

"About what?"

"About something important."

Spyros glanced around the deck. "I'm expecting a call from Chicago," he said. "I'm still trying to unload that gray snapper. They're frozen, but I'm going out this week and need the space. I expect the call any minute. If Chicago won't take them, I'll have to call St. Louis or Kansas City."

I didn't want to stay on the wharf and shout, but I was determined to talk to him. He must have known how I felt, for he opened the gate at the head of the gangplank and motioned me aboard.

He walked to the stern of the ship, away from the bridge, where the radio operator stood watching us. As I followed him, he turned and smiled, the dazzling smile that always made my heart leap. It leaped now.

"What can I do for you, Alexandra?" he asked me.

"You can tell me the truth," I said.

There could have been some note in my voice. Or the way I glanced at him, enchanted once more by his godlike look.

"You know that I love you very much," he said. "If I were five years younger or you were not a child in school, I would race away with you to the ends of the earth. No one could stop me. I'd run through a forest on fire, if need be, with a wildcat under each arm."

I thought of saying, "And what would *I* be doing all this time, while we were running through a forest fire with wildcats?" Rather, I said, "After the storm I found two packets of cocaine on the boat, one of them hidden in a sponge."

I took a packet from my blouse and handed it to him. He held it to the light, opened it, wet his finger, and put a few of the powdery crystals on his tongue.

"Cocaine," he announced and spat it out on the deck. "Pure and uncut."

"Our sponges at the exchange are stuffed with cocaine," I said.

He appeared to be shocked. "Then you can't possibly sell them."

He said this solemnly, as if the very thought of selling them was abhorrent. Yet I felt that this wasn't exactly what he meant, that he had meant to say, "Then you can't possibly sell the sponges, *can you?*" and then for some reason had changed his mind.

"Not possibly," I said. "Not this time."

"What do you mean?"

"I mean we have sold sponges before at the auction, three times before, that were probably stuffed with cocaine."

"Who bought them?"

"George Kanarsis."

"Who's George Kanarsis?"

"All I know is that he's a manufacturer of perfume and lives in Miami."

"Never heard of him."

A plane with Coast Guard markings flew up the river, circled back, and headed toward Anclote Key. I watched it until it was out of sight. Silently, Spyros watched it, too.

"Where did the dope come from?" he asked. "How did it get on the boat?"

I paused, suddenly fearful of saying the wrong thing, of destroying any chance I had of getting at the truth.

"You must have some idea, Alexandra. An evil fairy didn't just fly down in the stillness of the night and insert neat little packages of cocaine in each of your sponges. You must have an idea about it."

"I do. The cocaine came straight from your ship."

Spyros laughed.

"That's the only place it could have come from," I said.

The radio operator called down from the bridge as Spyros started to answer me. He excused himself and disappeared. A short time later I heard him shouting on the phone.

Vapor rose from the river. It might have been steam. The river might have been on fire. A lone pelican stood on the rail with its beak open, trying to trap some of the burning air.

I wiped the perspiration from my face and took a deep breath. I felt unsure of the track I was following, less sure than I had been only a short time before.

Spyros came back, apologizing, to announce that he had sold the gray snapper to a firm in Kansas City. "I'll ship them off this afternoon and be on my way to Costa Rica in a couple of days. Before I leave, I hope I can help you in some way with your cocaine problem."

"You can," I said.

"How? You said a moment ago that the cocaine came from my ship. How could it? Did you see any of my crew bring it? If they did, they were walking on water. The dope couldn't get there without your knowing about it. Except when you were diving, you were on the boat night and day."

"Except," I said, "on the nights I was on *your* boat."

"In other words," he said calmly, "I'm responsible for the dope you found in the sponges. How ridiculous!"

"I am only saying that the cocaine was hidden on our boat while Grandfather and I were having dinner with you. That's all."

"Other boats were in the vicinity. The dope could have come from any one of them."

"There were none around two nights ago. Two nights ago," I said, "while I was on the bridge talking to my mother, I saw a trail of phosphorescence in the water. Your launch was making it on the way back from our boat."

Spyros pondered these words for a while, then, deciding not to challenge me, he said, "The launchman might have delivered a package to your boat without ever knowing what was in it."

"The package might have come from a member of your crew."

"It's possible. Everyone in Florida and their brothers and aunts, sisters and cousins, seem to be in the drug business these days. Drugs are coming into the state by luxury liner, sailboat, motorboat, fishing smack, rowboat, by plane, helicopter, and balloon, sewed in the hatbands of men, hidden very privately by women, in children's Barbie dolls and rattles. It's one helluva mess."

"If drug running is as common as you say it is, then some of your crew may be in it."

"Let me do a little sleuthing. In the meantime, go ahead and sell your stuff at the auction. The cocaine doesn't belong to you. You know nothing about it. You didn't buy it. You're not selling it. You're selling a batch of sponge."

"That's dangerous," I said, trying to sound innocent, appearing as though I was willing to go along with him.

"You'll be safe. The Feds are down in Casey Key."

I wondered how he knew that the federal agents were seventy miles away, in Casey Key.

"Besides, no one in his right mind would ever suspect Alexandra Dimitrios of peddling dope."

"That may be why they chose our boat to run the stuff in."

"Of course. For no other reason. Listen, my dear, you can't afford to turn sponge over to the Coast Guard and lose hardearned money. Next week you'll be back in school, diving only on weekends. With winter coming and the weather getting tricky, not always on weekends. The family has paid off its debts, or so Daphne tells me, but you'll need money and won't have it."

He waited for me to answer. When I was silent, he added something more. But two fishing boats were coming in from the sea. The crews were cleaning the fish and throwing the offal into the river. Gulls were fighting over it. I heard nothing except their screams.

Spyros strolled toward the gate and I followed him. He was shepherding me off the ship, smiling all the while from under the brim of his fisherman's cap. He never looked more handsome. Once more he was the sea god Poseidon, dark from sun and wind and long days spent in his watery kingdom. Once more I felt my heart cease to beat and I thought that in all this world it would never beat again.

He crimped the packet of cocaine and handed it back, saying that it was vicious stuff. As I tossed it over the rail, the pelican quit gasping for breath and caught it in midair.

"I think we've made a beginning," Spyros said. "You feel better about everything now. When you came on board you were scared to death."

I was still scared. I smiled, but it was difficult.

"I'll do some work and report what I find," he repeated. "Sell the sponge at the auction, but from now on, take care. It's dangerous business. You've brought cocaine in before — the Feds could haul you up for that."

The sun beat down. I was standing on a metal cover that burned through the soles of my shoes. He was bullying me now, staring at me with his dark eyes. I moved away. As I did so I heard a sound. I thought it came from the deck cover, sliding under my weight. Then I realized that a car door had closed. I heard a burst of country music.

Spyros stepped past me to the rail and glanced down. The music stopped.

"Hey there, Captain," Tasso called out. "Steve and me are off to Tampa and we need some dough. Five hundred bucks will do all right."

Spyros made a quick motion with his head. Tasso mumbled a reply. I heard his heavy tread on the wharf and the radio play again.

For a moment or two Spyros' expression didn't change. There was no sign that Tasso had been there asking for money, shouting words that clearly linked Spyros to the cocaine that sat in the courtyard of the Sponge Exchange.

He closed the gate, and as he turned toward me his expression suddenly changed. He was standing with his back against a pile of green chafing gear, and the sun's reflection gave his skin a greenish cast. Yet it could not have transformed his face into the mask that now stared out at me.

"You've heard about Daphne and me," he said. "You and I will soon be brother and sister. I'll be a member of your family and you'll be a member of mine. Greek families stick together, as you know. They are loyal to each other. What hurts one, hurts all. That's the way it was in Greece for centuries and that's the way it is in Tarpon today."

He was speaking, or trying to, as if we were already brother and sister, Greeks against a common enemy. Yet there was a tone in his voice that I found vaguely sinister.

"Don't you believe so?" he asked me.

"Yes," I said. "I believe that families should be loyal to each other. I believe also that each person in the family should be loyal to his or her own self."

"That sounds a little complicated."

"It *is* complicated."

Somehow I suddenly felt threatened. I excused myself and opened the gate and went down the gangplank. Tasso was at the car, leaning in with his radio going, to say something to Parsons. I untied the boat. The pelican that had swallowed the packet I'd thrown in the river was floating along on its side, feebly flapping its wings.

# ❧ 23

Grandfather was still at the Acme Ice Cream Parlor, talking with the two waitresses and working on his second Idiot's Delight. He was so occupied that he didn't look at me as I sat down at the table, ordered a dish of plain vanilla ice cream, and waited for him to finish his story about the big hurricane.

One of the waitresses was called away and at last, looking at the one who was left, he said, "Where have you been, Alexandra? You had me worried."

No worry was visible.

"Across the river talking to Spyros," I said.

"About what was the talk? The wedding?"

"In a way."

This was the truth. In a way we had talked about the wedding. It lay at the heart of Spyros' last words. They still rang in my ears, word upon word.

"You think well of it?" Grandfather asked. "The Papadimitrioses and the Stavaronases?"

"Daphne is in love," I said. "That's important."

"That is good. Love is good." He frowned. "But the father of Herakles Stavaronas, he who murdered Jews — the women, the children — this Stavaronas sticks in my throat."

The waitress was doing something at the next table and listening to us. Grandfather decided to speak in the language of Kalymnos.

"But I have come to like Spyros," he said, "and you like him also. You have liked him for a long time, since the night of the big celebration with all the spongers. Your eyes sparkled that night. I had never seen them sparkle so before. But they are not sparkling now, Aliki. Now they have the look of a diver who comes up after being down in the deeps too long. You've just been talking to Spyros. Have you changed your mind about him?"

It was hard to smile and look happy, to conceal the turmoil that still had a grip on me, but I tried.

"Wonderful," Grandfather said, accepting my feeble efforts. "So we have a big wedding. Tomorrow after the auction we send the invitations, we invite everybody, friends and enemies, Stavaronases and Papadimitrioses, everybody."

As I sat there listening to Grandfather plan the wedding, all I could think about was Spyros Stavaronas, dealer in drugs, who was shipping cocaine bought in Colombia or Panama — somewhere on his shrimping expeditions — and using us and our boat to bring it into the United States. That now, at this moment, while we sat in the ice cream parlor, our cargo of sponge on display in the courtyard of the Sponge Exchange was stuffed with packets of cocaine.

"I'm going back to school next week, remember? I'll have only Saturdays to dive. And not then if the weather's bad, which it will be most of the time. The auction money has to last."

"Can you keep a secret?" Grandfather asked, leaning across the table and lowering his voice. "I have money."

"I know you have money. It's in the hole you dug in the garage. But that has to last us all winter."

"Not that money. Other money."

"What other money?"

"The money I saved the years when I was the best diver in all the Middle Gulf."

It took me a moment to collect myself. "You mean that the day we gathered in the kitchen after Father's funeral, and Mother said we had debts we couldn't pay, and you agreed and said that the only way we could pay them was for us, the two of us, to go to the Gulf and dive for sponge . . ."

"I recall."

"And all the time you had money hidden away in that hole in the garage floor?"

He gave me a grandfatherly look, as much of a look as he could with the tremors he had in both of his eyes that made his eyelids flutter open and close most of the time. "If I'd had a grandson it would have been easier. As it was, I had to settle for the talent that was at hand."

"A girl. Me, Alexandra. Thanks for very little. Thank you very much for nothing."

"Not nothing. In five years you would be a fine diver, better each year, diving deeper and deeper in the dark waters. But you'll not dive for five years more. Nor for one year more, probably. But this summer you have proven yourself in a way that you never could by winning medals in the breaststroke."

"I like medals."

"Everyone likes medals. The trouble is, there aren't nearly enough medals to go around. So most of the young are left out, all except a handful. And medals are not the point, after all."

"I worked hard for my medal, though it was only a bronze," I said, seeing Spyros as he looked down at me from the ship's rail, feeling now a sudden sharp pain at the thought of Spyros in trouble.

Grandfather nodded. "And likewise it took patience and self-denial and courage. You've heard the familiar list of virtues from your coach and from the mayor who presented the medal. But winning a medal for a swim in the river is not like diving for sponge in the deep waters. One is trivial and one is not. It is this that makes the difference."

Staring at my ice cream, which had melted, I had only a vague idea of what he was getting at.

"Nothing looks more awful," I said, "than a dish of melted vanilla ice cream."

I wasn't listening to him very much and he wasn't listening to me at all, which was customary. "You're lucky," he said. "Not every girl has faced the deep waters. You have, Aliki, and learned much. What you have yet to learn is that the deepest waters are not out in the Gulf but somewhere deep inside you. And you will learn this as you have learned the other."

"I suppose so," I said, my thoughts fixed upon Spyros Stavaronas.

As we got up to leave, one of the waitresses asked for my autograph. The parlor was crowded with tourists, and when word got around that I was a sponge diver, they surrounded me. I autographed six napkins, two calling cards, the backs of five letters, a T-shirt with the legend TARPON SPRINGS, SPONGE CAPITAL OF THE WORLD, and the bill of a man's cap before I could get out of the place. Signing my name should have given me a thrill, but it didn't.

## ❧ 24

We went down to the boat, Grandfather hobbling along at my side. Parsons' red car was still parked across the river, between the entrance to the packing house and the shrimper. I mentioned the car to Grandfather.

"We'll have to pay him for the rifle," he said. "The one you threw in the sea. They don't come cheap, the thirty-ought-sixes."

"Gladly," I said.

"And then he'll buy another gun, perhaps a machine gun next time."

"But he won't bring it on the boat, ever."

Tasso was on the shrimper at this moment, pocketing the money he had asked for while I was there.

The red car pulled away, tires squealing, radio blaring, and disappeared on the road to Tampa. Spyros would be pacing the deck now with his long, graceful strides — he couldn't think without pacing. What were his thoughts? What would he decide to do? He was not a mere accomplice, like Tasso and Parsons. He was Spyros Stavaronas, the man in charge of the drug operation, the one who would suffer the most if he were caught.

My last moments on the ship were a clue to what he might decide. He had turned his dark gaze upon me, certain in the belief that I was still in love with him, that he had the power to control my every thought and action.

Sea gulls were cruising the river. White pelicans sat on the wharf and watched, waiting until the gulls turned up something of interest. Stretching out on the deck in the only patch of shade, Grandfather left a request that he not be bothered for an hour at least.

I looked at him lying there, his weathered face serene and proud in the knowledge that he had done what he had set out to do. He had proven that he was not a helpless old man stumbling around in everyone's way, an object of patience and pity. Lacking a grandson, he had also proven, through me, that the proud blood of ancient Kalymnos had not turned to water. The discovery that he was part of a drug operation, though an innocent part — an unsuspecting dupe — would hurt him deeply.

I left the boat and walked down Dodecanese to the Sea Grotto, where Daphne worked. I had promised to go with her when she tried on her wedding dress. The curio shop was crowded with tourists buying stuffed fish, baby alligators, seashells, pieces of driftwood, and five-dollar sponges that the divers had sold for fifty cents. But Daphne walked out through the crowd and we went across the street to the department store.

The long dress was white, with full sleeves and a bodice that rose to a bateau neckline. The clerk held it up and turned it around and around under the lights while Daphne murmured ecstatically.

The clerk and Daphne went into the dressing room to put on the gown. I stood and looked at myself in the mirror. Then I went to the door and looked out at the river, at the gulls flying and at the sponge boats going by. When I came back, I had made up my mind.

Daphne would be stricken, yet I believed, putting myself in her place, that it was better for her to suffer pain now than later, tied to a man who had little to offer her through the years except unhappiness.

Grandfather would be shocked, then embarrassed, then angry at himself for thinking good of any member of the Stavaronas family. But in time he, too, would forget.

As for Spyros, he was still a romantic figure to me, still a part of a summer's dream, but he was no longer the sea god Poseidon. He was in a dirty business that preyed upon the weaknesses of people. He deserved to go to prison.

Daphne came back dressed in the white gown with the bateau neckline. She had brought a pair of high-heeled shoes with her and had put them on, white shoes with pearl buttons. She looked like a princess, as beautiful as her namesake, the Greek nymph Daphne.

She had mussed her hair when she was getting into the

dress and asked me to bring her a comb from her bag. While I was fishing around in the bag, I happened upon a small plastic packet exactly like the packets I had found on the boat. I held it to the light. Inside the transparent wrapping was a tube of white cocaine.

I closed the bag and took Daphne her comb and watched her comb her hair, which was long and fell on her shoulders and curled up like a wave breaking.

"What about your dress?" she asked me. "You're the bridesmaid. With your blond coloring you'll look nice in some shade of pink."

"Yes," I said, "in some nice shade of pink."

"We should order it now. If we don't, it won't be ready in time."

"I have things to do on the boat," I said. "I'll come back with you later."

Daphne looked in the mirror, admiring herself — her bodice, her slim waist, the high-heeled shoes with rows of glistening pearls. Then she turned and looked at me.

"You're quiet," she said. "You're not unhappy about Spyros and me, are you?"

"No," I said.

"I thought you might be since you've been going around all these months with a mad crush on him."

I was silent, letting her think what she wanted to.

"Cheer up! You're very young. Someday you'll find someone you're just as crazy about as you are about Spyros Stavaronas. Smile, Alexandra. You're pretty when you smile."

I smiled to please her and said goodbye.

As I walked toward the river, I kept thinking about the packet of cocaine I had found in her bag. I was more certain now than before that I was making the right decision.

Daphne wasn't the only one in our school who used cocaine. Five students, three girls and two boys, had been busted during the last semester. There were more than that who hadn't been caught. You could buy the stuff at one of the curio stores, or so I had heard. Now there would be less to sell in Tarpon Springs and elsewhere.

# ❧ 25

It was noon and the Coast Guard station was closed for lunch. I waited for an hour before Petty Officer Rogers drove up and parked her car. She opened the door and eyed me as if to say, "Are you here again?"

The office was dark and hot and smelled of flowers. She opened the curtains that had been drawn against the sun and sat down at her desk, which was covered with papers. At one side of the desk stood a tall vase with a bunch of beautiful red roses neatly arranged.

"If you've come to ask about Captain Stavaronas," she said, "his ship has docked across the river. You'll find him aboard."

"I am not here to ask about Captain Stavaronas."

"You were here before to ask. Early in the summer."

"Are you interested in information about smuggling?" I asked her.

"What kind of smuggling?"

"Cocaine."

"What do you wish to report?"

She glanced at me, and her eyes were cold. I remembered that they had been cold before, the first time I had come to ask about Spyros, and afterward. She had gone out of her way to make me look like a foolish schoolgirl.

"What is it?" she said impatiently, shuffling the papers on her desk. "I am very busy."

Her voice was as cold as the look she then fixed upon me. At that moment I knew something I should have known long before — that she herself was in love with Spyros Stavaronas. I wondered if he had given her the roses.

She took up a pen and scribbled a few words on a pad. Then her icy blue eyes rested on me again.

"Well?" she said, her pen poised in the air.

I started to speak, said a few words, and stopped. What, I asked myself, would become of the facts I was about to reveal? In love with Spyros Stavaronas, would she call his ship when I left the office and tell him everything I had told her?

The pen was still poised. Her eyes were still boring into me, icy cold. I remembered that the Coast Guard headquarters were located in Tampa. I had been there once with my father. Mumbling an excuse — I don't know what it was — I thanked her. I closed the door behind me and fled.

Grandfather was asleep when I got back to the boat. I turned on the motor and took in the mooring lines. We passed the shrimper lying at the Stavaronas wharf. I didn't look to see if Spyros was on the bridge.

After we had left our pier far astern Grandfather woke up. He rubbed his eyes and began to study the passing shoreline.

"Where in the devil's own name do you take me?" he growled.

"To Tampa," I said.

He reached for the tiller. "Why do we go to Tampa? Why there? Do you have flies in your head?"

I took a firm grip on the tiller and held the boat on course. Two planes roared over us, headed for the Gulf, both of them carrying the Coast Guard insignia. I waited until the roar died away and the river was quiet, then I told him the whole story, taking my time, starting with the day we sold our first load of sponges to George Kanarsis. Everything except the packet I had found in Daphne's purse.

Through it all, Grandfather was sitting on the stern thwart, his back turned to me. I didn't see his face. He never moved and never uttered a word until I had finished. Then a groan escaped him, and I felt a violent tremor run through his body.

"Tampa is two long hours away," he said. "Many things can happen in two hours. If Parsons and Tasso find out that you've discovered the cocaine, they might have time to steal the sponge from the auction and disappear. Stavaronas himself could steal the stuff. The only evidence against him is there in the courtyard. We should go back and call the Coast Guard from home."

"If we call from home, the news will be all over the county in ten minutes. We have a party line, and the line has a dozen numbers and an operator who's connected to all of them and loves gossip."

"We can call from Tarpon."

"Then everyone knows the news in half that time, in just five minutes."

Grandfather turned slowly and glanced back at the town we were leaving. "We'll cause a lot of trouble and grief," he said. "People like to have the law enforced, but not when the law is against them and their friends."

Had he changed his mind? I wondered. Perhaps I was wrong in believing that he wouldn't hesitate to report the crime. Had he considered all that I had told him and decided that the bad outweighed the good? Officers were hired to enforce the law and run down criminals. As bystanders, as people who were not responsible for the crime, did he think it best for us to stay out of it, to remain silent?

He turned and looked ahead, at the river and the sea shining in the sun.

It doesn't matter what he thinks, I said to myself, and set a course for the Coast Guard station in Tampa.

A gray bird with a long neck and legs trailing like sticks flew over and cocked its head at us. A shrimper passed, going west to the fishing grounds. As we reached open water at Anclote Key a fair wind was blowing.

I had already put up the mainsail. Then Grandfather hobbled forward and set the little trisail we always used when we were in a hurry.